COME INTO THE SUN
Tropical Escape, Book Two

BARBARA MCMAHON

Come Into The Sun
Copyright © 2012 Barbara McMahon
All Rights Reserved

1

Alexis Kent sat on the cord-bound box at the edge of the long weathered pier, near the ramp leading to the sloop, her old surplus army duffel bag bulging beside her. Her denim tote rested on the pier near her small box. The sun was high in the West Indies sky; the air still; and the creaking of mooring lines, and the murmur of the small wavelets slapping against the planking of a dozen boats, a mellow background for the crying sea-gulls circling lazily in the sky. In the distance, on the commercial dock, old men were repairing their fishing nets, sitting unconcerned with the burning rays of the hot sun.

She shifted her position a little. Not fidgeting, outwardly serene and patient, only moving to gain a new view. Waiting beside the large sloop mentioned in the advertisement, she could see the entire ship. The dark-blue hull of the ocean-going vessel gleamed brightly in the harsh sunlight, freshly cleaned and shining. The low cabin amidships shown a bright white. The porthole windows sparkled. All gear was stowed away; the teak deck carried no clutter. The jib sail was folded tidily by the bow rail, the mainsail tucked neatly in its cover along the center boom.

A wander-class sloop, almost forty feet at a guess. Lexy had studied it earlier, the narrow deck surrounding the cabin, the cut-out well in the stern at the wheel, enabling the skipper to stand or sit while at the helm. She had not boarded the boat, so did not know the cabin configuration. There would be the basics, she was sure; galley, head, sofa converting to bunks, perhaps a forward cabin with bunks. She shrugged—she'd find that out soon enough if she got the job.

She'd been sitting for over an hour. She'd called out upon arriving beside the sloop but received no answer. She'd plopped down to await the owner's return--still holding the paper in hand. She clutched it for reference, for introduction, and as a talisman. She really wanted this job.

It was hot and she grew thirsty in the unrelenting sun. How much longer?

Vaguely, her gaze touched on the old men working, talking among themselves; moving to watch the gulls, their circling flights, their dives. Some birds bobbed placidly on the water, resting. Was it cooler for them? She wished she could cool off in the water, not here in the harbor, but on a nice beach somewhere.

Her gaze moved to shore, diverted by the arrival of a taxi. A tall man climbed out of the cab, paid the fare, and started down the pier. She watched as he approached. Maybe he was the man she was awaiting. He was six feet tall at an estimate and solidly built. Dark brown hair, worn rather long, brushed the collar of his shirt and as he drew closer she saw his hair was flecked with gray. His eyes were a startling blue in the mahogany of his face, matching the knit shirt he wore. A square jaw and firm lips gave evidence of a determined, yet controlled individual.

As he drew closer, Lexy stood up, drawing his eyes, forcing him to really notice her for the first time. A small zephyr of air skipped by, cooling her a moment, before the hot glare of the sun resumed its boiling effect. He drew even with her and the ramp to the ocean-going sailboat.

'Mr. Frazer?' She did not quite reach his shoulder.

'Yes?' His glance was cool, registering, she knew, a small, thin woman. Her mop of short light brown hair was liberally streaked with blonde by the sun, her skin a deep honey gold, evidence of many hours in the open. She wore khakis and a sleeveless white T-shirt, her concession to appropriate attire for an interview for a job on a sailing ship. Tennis shoes clad her feet. She saw him flick a glance at the denim bag, which hung from her shoulder, and the old army surplus duffel at her feet. She met his gaze candidly.

'I'm Alexis Kent, Mr. Frazer. I've come about the crewman's job. Has it been filled?' She offered the square piece of paper she had pulled from the hotel board advertising the position of general crewman for an oceangoing sailing-sloop, Jack-of-all-work, experience required, apply at the Marybeth, Santa Inez Harbor.

He raised an eyebrow and glanced at the paper. 'The job hasn't been filled, but you won't do.' He passed her and lithely crossed the short ramp to the boat, landing on the deck as softly and sure-footed as a cat.

She turned and watched him a moment, raising her voice slightly. 'I'm experienced Mr. Frazer. And . . . and I'm very strong.'

Maybe it was her size that was off-putting, she thought hopefully. Fully aware, however, that it was her gender more than anything that kept her from the job; from even being considered for this job.

He turned at her voice as if surprised she was still there. At her assertion she was very strong a hint of amusement crept into his eyes, though his face remained sober. 'I'm sure you are, Miss . . . er. . . Kent, was it? I must confess, I thought I'd have better response to the ad. I posted it several days ago and you're the only applicant thus far. But you still won't do.'

She stared at him, trying to come up with something that might change his opinion, to give her a chance.

He remained watching her with a steadfast gaze that was disconcerting.

She sighed slightly in defeat and reached for her duffel bag and box. 'I'm at the Markly if..' If what? If he should change his mind? 'If you can't get anyone else.'

The Markly was a hangout for sailors, fishermen and cargo handlers on Santa Inez Island. A wild bunch on Saturday nights, and not much better the rest of the time. The hotel was close to the docks, though, and clean and cheap, it had been on an announcement board that Lexy had seen the posted ad for the job. Posted several days ago, as he had said. She took some satisfaction in knowing she was the only applicant thus far.

Not that it would do any good if he wouldn't seriously consider her for the job. She shook her head as she walked back up the pier. It wasn't fair, just because she was a woman. She paused at the street and glanced back. Dominic Frazer had turned and was gazing out to sea, not giving her another thought. With a regretful sigh, she continued her way back towards the hotel.

Idiot, she thought angrily as the duffel bag banged rhythmically against her leg. I should not have counted on the job, just because I have experience. How silly he must think me to show up all packed and ready to go. It was stupid. I should have first made sure I obtained the position, then packed up. Blast the man anyway for not even giving me a token interview.

She stopped and let her duffel and box down slowly. Flexing her fingers to ease the strain, she picked them up changing hands this time, and continued.

It was hot. Perspiration trickled down her back and between her breasts. The way back to the hotel seemed longer and harder than the walk to the marina.

She was most anxious to leave Santa Inez, escape as she put it, to get as far away from the uncomfortable situation with the Culvers as she could. To get away and start anew where no one knew her or anything about her or her past life. Where people would believe whatever she had to tell them, not be prejudiced by past events, not be influenced by rumors and gossip and unfounded allegations. Especially about something that had happened so long ago. She had so been looking forward to this position.

Something else would turn up. She just needed to be alert to opportunities and be ready to act when they arose.

Two days later, late in the afternoon, Lexy Kent wandered into the bar at the Markly Hotel, discouraged and hot, grateful to lean her arms against the cool polished wood of the bar. The room was dim, shaded and sheltered from the intense heat, a slow-moving ceiling fan swirling the air a little. Not really cool, but at least giving the impression of coolness--a welcomed relief from the broiling afternoon sun.

'Hi, Dick,' she said, greeting the man behind the bar. 'I'll have a large lemonade, plenty of ice, please.'

The dark old man behind the counter smiled sympathetically, his white teeth flashing in the faint light. 'Bad day, Lexy?' he asked as he filled her glass.

'You said it. I can't find a job anywhere! I shouldn't have left my other one until I had something else lined up. Ummm, that's great.' She tilted her head and drank deeply from the lemonade-filled glass.

'Gentleman over there asking for you,' Dick said in a low voice, nodding across the room towards a table on the far side. Lexy Kent turned slowly, her face apprehensive. It cleared at once seeing Dominic Frazer tilted back in a chair, a tall lager on the table before him. He watched her.

She took her glass and walked calmly over, her face smiling politely. 'Mr. Frazer. Dick said you were asking for me. May I?' She pulled out a chair and waited.

Dominic Frazer banged down his chair on all four legs and nodded. Lexy sat and waited—it was only a moment before he spoke, yet the time dragged by. Lexy was conscious of his appraising regard, his cool, blue eyes. She was curious as to why he was here, but tried not to show it. Calmly she met his gaze and waited for him to begin. He had asked for her after all, not the other way around, so he could begin the conversation.

'Are you still interested in the position on my boat?' he asked at last.

Her face lit up, but her reply was a rather guarded, 'I am.'

'I seem to be having trouble attracting applicants. I want to sail soon and need a second person. The sloop has been moored here on the island for the last six months. Now I'm ready to take off. My problem is my brother's always crewed for me in the past, but he was married recently and is now working in Barbados.' Dominic Frazer shook his head impatiently. 'If I had had any idea of how difficult it would prove to hire someone here, I would have filled the position when I was in Bridgetown. Tell me, Miss Kent, why do you want the job?'

'I rather need it,' she began slowly, choosing her words carefully. 'I came here in the employ of ... of someone, and when my services were no longer required, naturally I began looking for another job. I thought I'd like something I had done before. I have been most recently working as a cook, but didn't like it as much as I thought I would. I like being outdoors, not stuck in a hot kitchen all the time. I've sailed extensively on several different kinds of boats. There aren't many jobs going right now, yours looked suitable.' She turned her glass absently on the table before her, watching her fingers tracing patterns in the condensation. 'I'm ready to leave Santa Inez, too,' she added, shrugging off that reason.

He raised his eyebrows at this, but asked no questions. 'So you can cook?' he asked.

'Oh, yes, I'm a good cook,' she replied enthusiastically, on safe ground at last. 'I've sailed on a ketch and a seafarer-class sloop. I know a little about navigation and how to judge the currents and winds of the Caribbean. Not enough to do it on my own, though,' she added truthfully, 'where are you heading?'

He smiled at this. 'Do you care?' he asked. 'As long as it's away from here?'

She grinned impishly. She watched his eyes move to the small dimple showing in her right cheek. For a moment she remembered another man, another time. 'Got it in one. Anywhere is fine with me. I'm footloose and fancy free.'

He glanced at his lager, his eyes hooded, unreadable. 'I'm a writer, Miss Kent. I've been doing research the last few months and am now getting down to writing the book. I want no distractions, no interference. I plan to sail out to sea, anchor and get on with it.' He paused, glancing up to gauge her reaction. She watched him steadily. Seemed extreme to her, but she'd always heard writers were quirky.

'I need a crewman who can pull his own weight.' He smiled tightly at this, his glance going quickly over her slight frame. 'I would also like someone to cook, keep the ship tidy, but most of all someone who can entertain himself—or in your case herself—not disturb me while I write. It'll be a rather lonely existence, I'm afraid—no town, no bright lights, no beauty parlors.' He stopped, quirked an eyebrow in silent question, waiting for her reply.

Lexy nodded. 'Do I really look like I frequent a beauty parlor?' Her hair was tousled, cut short by the nearest barber and totally sun- streaked. She wore no make-up. Her eyelashes were dark, her skin was tanned dark brown by the sun. She preferred healthy to artifice.

Abruptly he asked, 'Tell me, what do your parents think of your trying for such a job?'

That question caught her by surprise. Just how old did he think she was?

'My parents are both dead, Mr. Frazer. They have been for many years,' she replied quietly. "And if they were alive, they'd have little say on how I make a living.' She was annoyed by his change of subject and the manner in which he asked his question as if she needed permission to do something. But she didn't show it. She'd learned long ago to keep her reactions to herself.

'Surely they'd be concerned with you going off for maybe months at a time?' He wouldn't be put off.

She was surprised at this. 'Just how old do you think I am? I haven't answered to anyone for a long time.'

'Nineteen, maybe twenty.' He replied to her question, assessing her trim figure, her clear eyes and smooth skin.

She gave him a beautiful smile, her eyes warm and friendly, her dimple showing again. She took a quick sip of lemonade. 'You've made my day! I'm twenty-six. I sometimes feel a hundred and six, but never nineteen!'

She saw his surprise and the look of disbelief growing on his face. Wryly she shook her head. 'The light, or lack of it in here, must flatter. I have my passport, and several letters of recommendation upstairs showing the years I've worked. I assure you I'm older than you think.'

'My compliments, Miss Kent, you carry your years well. That solves one complication. I'll check your references that refer to your sailing experience. Then I have a proposition to make.'

Lexy did not stiffen nor shy away from his suggestion as many women might have done with the particular word he used, but her eyes did narrow and she watched him warily. She saw with satisfaction that he noticed her change of manner, was aware of her slight withdrawal, though he made no comment on it.

'We sail tomorrow for Bridgetown. I have a few things I want to pick up there before going . . . er. . . incommunicado. I'll try you out until we reach Barbados. You can see how you like it as well. If either of us doesn't wish to continue the association beyond Barbados, we'll agree to part, no bad feelings.'

She considered it a moment, and nodded. 'A good plan, captain, I agree. I'll get my references. Do you need to see my passport as well, for the age and all? I really am twenty-six.' The fat would be in the fire if he said yes. She bit her lip waiting his reply, her mind whirling with excuses and explanations should he want to inspect her passport, too. She hoped he wouldn't.

He leant back, tipping his chair. 'The letters will do.'

Lexy gulped down the last of her drink in relief and left the bar. Once out of sight of Dominic Frazer she gave a hop and a jump. She had it; she just knew she had the job. She paused as a flicker of doubt assailed her. Well, maybe she had it and maybe it would be a good job. The only question—would Dominic Frazer be like so many of his brethren and expect more from his new crewman than only ship work? That thought quenched some of Lexy's enthusiasm, but she shrugged it off. It was less than a week's sail to Barbados, she could fend him off for a week if need arose. They'd do different stints at the wheel, easy enough to stay out of his way the rest of the time. She'd try it, anyway. If it didn't work out, she'd at least be in Barbados and in a much better position to seek new employment than in tiny, out of the way Santa Inez.

Reaching her room she crossed quickly to the duffel to dig out the references. She took the treasured letter from Miles that would be the best, the one dealing with sailing experience. She hesitated over Mrs. Culver's; while not warm or inspiring, she had truthfully stated Lexy's talent in the culinary field. Yes, she would take that one down, too. The others—she shook her head, they wouldn't be any good. These two would have to do.

She turned to leave, then turned back, checking herself in her mirror. Her hair was tossed about, a warm flush on her cheeks attested to the heat of the day. She grabbed her brush, dragging it through the unruly curls. When some order had been restored, she pulled a face at herself and left. She had no wish to look too glamorous for the job, she told herself. This was strictly business, nothing more.

Lexy sat calmly at the table while Dominic perused the recommendations. The one from Miles Jackson was long and detailed, describing all her accomplishments and abilities. Dominic obviously recognized the signature, and he looked up at Lexy consideringly for a long moment. Laying that missive aside, he quickly read Mrs. Culver's much shorter letter. Folding them both along their original creases, he held them a moment, tapping them gently against the table's edge, lost in thought. Lexy wondered what he was thinking about, wondered what his decision would be.

'You'll do after all,' he said gravely, handing her back the papers. 'We'll sail on the tide, about eight tonight. Can you be ready?'

'Yes. And thank you, Mr. Frazer. I can come to the ship within an hour, if you like, or I can wait until later.'

'Come after dinner, save yourself one meal to fix. But be sure to come early enough to help make way.'

'I'll be there by seven.' She stood as he did, conscious once again of his height and size. A good man to have on your side if in difficulties. As she watched him leave she shivered. Probably a bad man to cross. She shook off her apprehension. Why should she even think about that? Gliding happily over to the bar, she smiled at the old barman as he wiped his glasses in solitary silence. The main customers of this bar were still earning their pay. After dark it filled up rapidly.

'I've got a job, Dick, I got it just now with that man, Mr. Frazer.' She waved towards the door through which Dominic Frazer had departed.

'Well that is good news, Lexy. Does it include a place to stay? Or will you be staying with us a little longer?'

'No, I have a place to stay, it's on a ship and I'm off to Barbados.' She smiled at the thought. While Barbados did not hold good memories for her, quite the opposite, in fact, she looked on the voyage as a new beginning. She was leaving Santa Inez, and this time things would be different!

'Well, sorry I will be to have you go, but it's best. You're too much a lady to be in a place the likes of this one.'

Lexy's face sobered as she glanced around, some of her joy dimmed. 'I haven't been a lady for a long time, Dick. This place's fine, it suited me and everybody here has been quite . . .' she hunted for the right word, 'proper.'

She shook off her mood, 'Anyway, I'm off tonight, so must pack and have a bite to eat. I'll say goodbye now, Dick, so that I don't have to do so when all the men are about.'

She extended her small, capable hand to the barman gravely shaking his.

'All the best Lexy,' he said gruffly.

Lexy was halfway up the stairs before she realized Dominic Frazer had not mentioned salary. Oh well, she shrugged, continuing to her room, the transportation to Bridgetown would be compensation enough if there wasn't more. Should they decide to continue after that, well, time enough to discuss salary later.

Dominique swung by the grocery store near the docks. He hadn't wanted to wait any longer to be under way, but he still had doubts about hiring a young woman to be his crew. If he could have made the trip alone, he would have and hired someone in Bridgetown.

Ordering enough supplies to last for the week's journey, and then some; he headed out to the post office. He'd send a letter home to alert them he was on his way. Then he'd swing by the bank and close that account. His time on St. Inez was over. He didn't plan to return.

So why was Lexy Kent so interested in leaving the island, he wondered. Money had to be tight or she could take a flight out. As he waited at a crosswalk, he thought more about her. She'd sure looked younger than she said she was. Maybe he should have checked her passport after all. Yet from the references, and the time she worked, she had to be older than a teenager. She didn't look it. She did look capable and determined. Attributes he himself liked. The shakedown cruise would show if she was as good as she said.

He stopped at the shrimp shack near the dock and got one last shrimp po'boy sandwich, and lots of fries. He'd miss this when he was gone. No facilities for french fries on the ship. The galley was small; most of the space would be filled with food. They'd eat their way through until they reached Barbados.

When he reached the sloop, he went aboard and began to reconfigure the interior cabin. He'd sleep on the fold down couch. He'd move his things from the lockers in the forward cabin, to give her room for her own things. He and his brother hadn't minded doubling up on their things. It would be different with someone else. Especially a woman. Though from what he remembered from earlier, she traveled light.

He couldn't believe no one else on the island came about the job. He'd posted it all over. Lexy Kent had been the only one to respond. Maybe the economy wasn't as bad as he thought. Or maybe no one wanted to leave St. Inez.

There'd be plenty of time to get to know his new crew member. If she suited–which he doubted–he'd keep her on. Otherwise, he'd find someone else once they reached home. He paused a moment thinking about his home and how long it had been since it had felt like a refuge. He planned a short visit. Appease the family, and then take off again. The memories would come, he had no doubt. But he would deal with them and shake them off once sailed away.

Lexy took advantage of her few remaining hours on St. Inez to soak in a long hot bath, washing her hair and pampering herself with lotions and creams. It would be a long time before she'd be able to enjoy such comforts. A quick dip in the sea and a rinse with fresh water would probably be her bath henceforth; bathing facilities were limited on an ocean sailboat.

Clean and fresh, dressed in the inevitable khakis and T-shirt, Lexy repacked her duffel bag. She carried all she owned with her and had pared down her belongings until they fit in the one bag. No dresses, Lexy didn't go places that required dresses. A jacket, folded at the bottom this time of year, khakis, shirts, shorts and a couple of swimsuits. Her underwear the only concession to femininity, being lacy and brief. Even her sleeping attire was merely large T-shirts, which fell to just above her knees.

The corded cardboard box, still bound up from her last move, contained about fifty paperback books. Lexy loved to read and gladly borrowed or exchanged whenever she could. The books changed, of course, as she found new ones and discarded old ones. A few she kept to reread, one she had for sentimental reasons, though she was loathe to admit that, even to herself. She had cut out sentimentality from her life—she had no time for it.

She put the duffel and the box by the door. She was ready. A quick dinner in the hotel's restaurant, early to miss most of the other inhabitants, and she'd head out. She'd told Dick the truth, as far as it went, everyone had been most proper around her. Still, she'd felt uncomfortable and conspicuous in the all-male gatherings at the hotel and would be glad to leave.

Dominic Frazer was on the deck of the sloop when she stepped onto the pier. He was checking lines, unsnapping sail covers and casually keeping an eye out for her.

Silhouetted by the late afternoon sun, her bag looking almost too big for her to carry, Lexy walked firmly toward the boat. She had had several spells of indecision during the afternoon, wondering if she'd done the right thing in hiring on, yet what choice did she have? She wanted to leave Santa Inez; this was the only job available. Though Barbados as a destination would not have been her first choice, it was a large enough place for her to find something more suited to her should this position not work out. She knew the places to avoid, the people not to run into, and if this didn't work, she'd be in a much better position to find a new job.

This had to work–at least for a week. She would see that it did.

The recommendation by Miles Jackson, a name familiar as a leading authority in marine biology in the Caribbean, had been most explicit in all the aspects of sailing and marine navigation in which Lexy was proficient. She wasn't worried about her abilities. Just her interactions with her new boss.

Dominic stopped work and watched her as she carried her things along the pier.

"You're prompt," he said, stepping down and offering a hand to help her aboard.

'Hello,' her soft voice floated across the water. It was low, serene and pleasing.

'Welcome aboard.' He reached for her bag, but Lexy shook her head.

'I can manage, if you'll tell me where to put it.' She took the short ramp in small running steps, landing near him on the narrow deck.

'Below, forward all the way. There's a small cabin, two bunks, it's yours.'

'And where will you sleep?' She paused; surely it wasn't going to end up impossible after all.

'The sofa in the main cabin drops down and makes a bunk, I'll use that. In the past, when my brother and I sailed the Marybeth, we shared the cabin. That, of course, under the circumstances, is no longer possible.' He spoke coolly, firmly.

Lexy went below with uplifted spirits. The sloop was spacious for a sailing ship. The short ladder-stairs, four in all, led to the main cabin. A compact galley was along the port side of the ship, next to the head. The other side had the sofa-cum-dining area arrangement. Ahead was the door leading to the small forward cabin. Lexy opened it and entered. It was narrower than the main cabin, of course, with two bunks on either wall, joining in a common headboard as the bow narrowed. Forward still, on the headboard, was a hatch leading to a triangular storage compartment. There were storage compartments beneath each bunk, as well as the standard ones in the main cabin and topside. Lexy dumped her gear on the port bunk, and taking a quick peek into the compartments, she saw Dominic's clothes in the drawers beneath that bunk. The corresponding space on the starboard side was empty.

That's mine, she thought, shifting her gear to the starboard bunk. Time enough later to unpack. She straightened and headed topside, noticing in passing that while the boat was not spanking new, it was well equipped and in excellent condition. Dominic Frazer obviously did not believe in denying himself a comfortable existence when 'incommunicado'.

With Lexy's help, they cast off a few minutes before eight, taking the ship out to sea with the mainsail only, using the steady offshore breeze. Once clear of the harbor, Dominic plotted the course and locked in on the coordinates for Barbados. They were on their way!

Lexy joined Dominic at the helm.

'You're experienced,' he commented, sitting back on the bench by the wheel, the ship steady on course. 'Did you sail a lot before working with Miles Jackson, Miss Kent?'

'No, but his Sea Tiger was not unlike this sloop, we used it a great deal for gathering data. Later he got a ketch and we used that.' She paused a moment, but Dominic did not pursue the topic. Lexy gave a silent sigh of relief. While her experience working with Miles had been an enjoyable period in her life, the reasons she'd had to leave were not.

'Mr. Frazer, since we will be together for several days, if not longer, would you like to drop Miss Kent and call me Lexy? It's my nickname and I like it better than Miss Kent.'

'Certainly, if you like.' He gave her a quick glance, but was apparently satisfied by what he saw. 'Call me Dominic.'

She nodded briefly, then turned her attention to the course laid in and the sea ahead. It was quiet, away from the land, almost silent –except for the slap of waves against the bow as they skimmed across the water. The sun dropped lower and lower in the sky, changing the color of the clouds on the distant horizon from bright pink to palest mauve. The trade winds were steady and strong enough to fill the sail. Long, slow swells were crossed easily by the running sloop. Behind them, Santa Inez island grew smaller and smaller, a dark mound diminishing in the evening sea, its sparkling lights growing dimmer until she could no longer see any.

'Who is she named for?' Lexy asked, curious about the ship.

'Who?' he asked, glancing at her.

'The ship.'

'She's the Marybeth, named for my wife,' he answered.

Lexy felt a small twinge of relief. He was married, well and good. She hoped he loved his wife and would constantly consider her, Lexy, as only a fellow sailor.

Still, she knew from Mr. Culver that having a wife did not stop a man with a wandering eye.

She threw a quick look in Dominic's direction. His own gaze was distant. His profile outlined against the setting sun; strong chin, aquiline nose, his hair moving a little in the breeze. She looked away, watching the prow rise and fall slightly. It wasn't surprising he was married. He was not very young, in his middle thirties she'd guess, obviously wealthy with a boat like this. She wondered briefly why his wife didn't accompany him. Perhaps she was too distracting when he was trying to write.

They sailed in silence, a peaceful, contented enjoyment of the quiet twilight, each lost in their own thoughts. Lexy jumped a little when Dominic switched on the running lights. She hadn't realized the sun was gone. Would he sail all night? Want her to take a watch? It would speed up their journey.

'You're a restful person, Lexy,' Dominic said in the growing darkness. 'You don't jabber all the time.'

She smiled at this, aware he couldn't see her. 'No, I guess I don't.' She turned to him. 'How do you want to work the watches tonight? Shall I sail her a bit while you sleep, do you want first watch, or what?'

'You go and sleep if you can. I'll sail till two or so, then you can take over.'

'Fine. See you then.' She rose and descended into the cabin. Before she turned on the light she stuck her head back out, 'Can I fix you coffee or something?'

'No, I'm fine. Goodnight.'

In the forward cabin Lexy took a few minutes to unpack her bag, utilizing the space beneath her bunk. Leaving her box of books for later, she slipped on her sleep shirt and crawled into the bunk. She set her watch for two and tried to sleep. She was alert to the chime of her watch, its soft insistence the only thing needed to bring her wide-awake. When she'd worked with Miles Jackson, they had usually worked different shifts and long hours, and she had developed the ability to drop off almost upon command. While it had been over two years since she had needed to, Lexy hadn't forgotten how, and she slept immediately. The small slapping sounds of the waves against the bow a monotonous soothing background, quiet and steady.

At two she awoke on the first note of her alarm. Quickly dressing, slipping on a heavy sweater for the cool tropic night, she stopped in the main cabin only long enough to fix herself a quick cup of instant coffee, before presenting herself topside.

'Lexy?'

'Hi, I've come to relieve you. Everything okay?'

'Everything's fine. I've marked our course, just checked the compass; the wind's steady. It's all yours.'

She looked over his chart, illuminated by a small red light, double-checked the compass and sat where he had been. 'Sleep well,' she said softly, gripping the wheel with her free hand.

When Dominic went below, she gave a sigh of pure delight as she sipped the coffee. She loved sailing and clear beautiful nights were her favorite. The moon was quartered and low on the horizon. The stars were plentiful, seeming so close Lexy wanted to reach out to try to touch one. The sea was a gray mysterious carpet, looking smooth, yet sending a thousand sparkling reflections back as it mirrored the stars, or made a shimmering path to the low moon.

Alexis loved sailing in the night, alone, but not lonely.

At peace with everybody and with herself. Forgetting all the hurts and pain of the last few years, feeling very much as a child again, loved, cosseted, sheltered. She loved sailing alone with only her thoughts and slowly the hours passed as the ship glided on the gray sea.

Dominic appeared on deck again shortly after seven, refreshed from his sleep, already washed and shaved. He scanned the sky, then wandered over to Lexy, checking the compass and looking at her.

'All right?' he asked.

She nodded. 'You want breakfast now?' as he sat beside her, enjoying the early morning coolness, the sun already warming the air.

'In a little while. Listen up so you don't get the wrong impression. I used the port bunk last night. I saw you had used the other. Since you were up here for the rest of the night, I used the bunk rather than making up the sofa bed. I won't use it when we are both sleeping at the same time—in port or at anchor. But

I didn't want you to get the wrong idea if you noticed the bunk had been slept in.'

She nodded. It made sense, as long as he didn't think they would share the forward compartment. It was his boat. He could do what he wanted.

They ran up the jib, catching all the wind they could, increasing the speed of the sloop. She stood braced against the slight swells and scanned the horizon. A clear beautiful day ahead. She grabbed her long-empty cup and went to fix their breakfast. Just as she was dishing up Dominic joined her in the cabin, shrinking the space, filling it with his presence.

'I'll eat here,' he said, sitting on the forward bench by the table. 'I've lashed the wheel and the wind seems steady.'

'Good.' Lexy placed their plates on the table and sat on the opposite bench, they both began eating. She kept her eyes on her food, not wanting to initiate conversation.

'As long as the wind holds and we stay course, there's no need for us to stay at the wheel all the time. Robin and I used to lock the wheel, then check the course every half-hour or so. You can feel if the wind changes or if the ship falters. At night, same thing, only we didn't sleep on watch in case we slept through the check time,' he said.

Lexy nodded, understanding. It would be advantageous to have a little more freedom, to let the locked wheel do its job and only check it to correct errors. She looked up to find Dominic staring at her, his blue eyes constantly surprising in the dark tan of his face.

'Do I have something on my face?' she asked, self-conscious from his regard.

'No. It wasn't the dim light in the bar, though. You still look like a teenager.'

She blushed very faintly and resumed eating, unsure of how to reply.

Dominic smiled faintly then glanced out of the porthole. 'I'll start preliminary outlines this morning as soon as the breakfast things are cleared away, if you'll take the watch. I'll come up this afternoon to take over.'

'Fine. It won't take me long to clean up.'

In less than half an hour Lexy finished eating, cleaned the cabin and changed into a bikini to wear topside. It was white, and brief. Her honey skin was evenly tanned all over, the bikini revealing her curves and valleys. The softly swelling breasts filling out the top, the brief pants rode low on her hips, smooth thighs tapering into slim calves. While not tall, her legs were long in proportion and nicely shaped. She took her sunscreen and sunglasses, then hesitated, wanting a book, but was disinclined to open her box if they would be parting company in Bridgetown. She shrugged, maybe Dominic would have something she could read.

Entering the main cabin, she found Dominic already in the midst of a pile of papers, jotting notes as he sorted through the data spread out before him, hunting for an elusive fact. Totally engrossed in what he was doing, he didn't notice Lexy by the edge of the table until she cleared her throat.

He looked up, scowling at the interruption. 'I said I wanted to work undisturbed,' he snapped.

She raised surprised eyebrows at his tone, contritely apologizing. 'I only wanted to see if you had a book I could read. I'm really sorry. I won't interrupt again.'

He frowned again, glancing at her attire, then turned back to his papers. 'In the compartment beneath the sofa, some books there. I'll call you when I want lunch.' He dismissed her and returned to his work.

Meekly she grabbed the first book in the drawer and hurried topside. He certainly meant it when he said he did not want interruptions.

Three hours later, Lexy was checking their course and correcting the wheel, and she glanced towards the cabin longingly. She was thirsty, but reluctant to annoy Dominic again. Tomorrow she would bring up a pitcher with something cool to drink, so as not to bother him during her watch. Shading her eyes until they adjusted to the interior light, she saw him still working hard, the steady click of the laptop a background for his writing. She bit her lip, deciding against going down for something, deciding against the risk of interrupting him a second time in one day. Tomorrow she'd plan better.

The book she'd snatched up was an absorbing mystery she hadn't read before. She was over half way finished. She looked at the number of remaining pages, not very many left now. Gazing out to sea, with the sun shining down on it, glittering on the restless water; sparkling and shimmering, the light bright and shining, she narrowed her eyes against the glare, scanning the horizon. In the far distance, off the port beam, she could see the outline of a large ship, too distant to tell if it were a cruise ship or freighter. Continuing her search, she saw nothing but a smooth horizon. They were alone in the vast sea, the ship on the port horizon even now growing smaller with each passing minute.

She looked at the water close at hand. It looked so inviting, so refreshing, that she wished she could go over the side. When she had worked for Miles, after hours of gathering data, they'd anchored and swum each day, combining diving for samples or photos with just plain frolicking in the warm Caribbean waters. Lexy rose slowly and wandered over to the lockers on the deck; looking into each one. In the third one she found flippers, face masks and snorkels. No scuba equipment, however. She replaced the lid and checked the fourth one—just marine gear. She hoped they'd find time for a swim even just a brief one.

Sitting back, leaning against the cabin wall, she idly watched the waves again, wondering if Dominic would stop at all before Bridgetown, or if he were in too great a rush to reach Barbados. She sighed. The day was pleasant and they would reach Bridgetown soon enough in any event. She reached for her book, soon lost again in the story, double-checking the clues leading to the denouement.

'Lexy!' A roar came from in the cabin.

She opened her eyes—at first unsure where she was. Recollection returned, she shook her head to clear it—she had dozed off. Rising stiffly, she quickly checked the sails, wheel and compass. They were fine, on course, and as she started to the cabin, she again heard Dominic's roar.

'Lexy!'

She started down the steep stairs. 'What?'

He turned to look at her, taking more notice of her brief bathing suit than he had earlier, grinning in appreciation. His mood friendly and relaxed. On the counter beside the sink were sandwiches-and a couple of cold beers.

'Lunch is ready,' he said, pointing to the food.

'Oh, I thought I was supposed to do that,' she said distressed. First day on the job and she had slept through mealtime.

'No problem, Robin and I often took turns. You'll have to eat standing up or on the sofa, I'm still working and didn't want to clear off the table.'

Lexy reached for a sandwich and turned to survey the scatter of papers surrounding the laptop. She thought it looked an unholy mess, but knew from working with Miles that the author probably knew exactly where everything was.

'Do you leave it like that while you work? All the time?'

Dominic looked at the table, then shrugged. 'Mostly,' he agreed.

'What do you write, what type of books? I haven't heard of any books by Dominic Frazer—do you write non-fiction?' she asked. She wanted to know more about her new boss.

He hesitated slightly, slanting her a glance from beneath his dark brows. Carefully he chose another sandwich, pausing, as if weighing whether or not to tell her. Finally, 'I write fiction, but not under my own name.'

'Why not?' She was surprised, her eyes narrowing suddenly, suspiciously, 'Unless you write trash and don't want to be associated with it?'

He looked a little embarrassed. 'Not really, but my work will never rival Shakespeare. My first book was written purely for the money. I wanted my name to be associated with something really good,' he gave a short laugh, shaking his head in remembrance. 'Anyway, it sold well and my publisher wanted more.' He shrugged. "So now I'm stuck with the name."

'So you kept writing books that sell and were stuck with your pen name. Is it a secret?'

'Lord, no, all my family and friends know what I do, who I am, so to speak. I'm only surprised the books keep selling so well.'

She fixed her gaze on him, still waiting for his pen- name.

Dominic cocked his eyebrow and grinned at her, still a trace embarrassed. 'Nick Roberts,' he obliged.

Lexy looked at him consideringly for a further minute, nodded, then reached for her second sandwich; they were good, the bread fresh and the meat tasty.

She took a bite and chewed it before speaking again. 'I've

read your books,' she said calmly, reaching for her beer and tilting her head back as she drank directly from the bottle.

Dominic waited, watching the smooth line of her jaw and throat, watching as she lowered the bottle and placed it back on the narrow counter.

She glanced up at him. 'They're good, that's why they keep selling,' she stated as a fact, not an opinion. Nodding to the cluttered table, she continued, 'Do you always research everything so thoroughly?'

'If you have read the books you'll remember they deal with different settings, different occupations. I have to research, I haven't traveled in the arctic, nor the Peruvian jungle, haven't been a Navy submarine captain, nor doctor.'

'If I've read them?' She smiled. 'I've read them, Dominic, all of them. You've written thirteen so far and I've read them all, they get better each time. Do you research the love angle, too?' For a moment she was flustered. 'Sorry, I forgot you were married, does your love angle come from your wife?'

His face became shuttered, his eyes hooded. He turned to the table, the camaraderie gone, his mood changed. 'My wife's dead,' he said flatly.

She stared at him, dumbfounded at her faux pas. 'I'm sorry. I didn't know,' she uttered softly, but wasn't sure he heard her. He gave no evidence he had heard or that he was aware she was still there. Eyes on his laptop screen, he typed, oblivious to his surroundings.

Regretfully, Lexy took another sandwich and her beer and went back on top. She should have asked about his wife before, found out something about her before teasing him about the love angle in his books. She wondered how long ago Mrs. Frazer had died. At least that explained why she wasn't on board, why Dominic had to hire a crew. She frowned in remembrance, had he said he was married, not had been? No, only that the boat was named for his wife.

She ate her sandwich slowly, thinking of Dominic and his dead wife. Her death must have been recent, and as he was still not used to her being gone, he hadn't made it clear that he was not married now. Idly she wondered what the dead Mrs. Frazer had been like, and she thought it unlikely that she'd ever know. Gradually she got over her embarrassment at the mistake. She would tread more warily in the future, but surely could be excused this one faux pas.

As she watched the sea, her spirits rose. Imagine she was working for Nick Roberts, one of her favorite authors. His adventure stories were very absorbing, his settings well illustrated and his characters exciting and believable. While it appeared he wrote primarily for men, his adventuresome heroes always accomplishing their objectives against fantastic odds, she liked the books. There was always a love element in them, adding to the appeal the basic story held. Some of the sex scenes were rather graphic, and the hero and heroine often didn't marry, but a happy, permanent ending was always the result. Knowing this did not detract from the books, the suspense was always gripping and enduring. What would this book be about, what would it be like? Would she get a chance to find out? Only if she stayed until he'd finished. Today hadn't been the best start, but Lexy was ever hopeful.

At four o'clock Dominic came up on deck. He spied Lexy lying in the slight shade of the cabin, and went to squat down beside her. 'The cabin's all yours when you want to fix dinner. I'd like to eat around seven, okay?'

'Fine.' She still felt awkward about her mistake at lunch but Dominic seemed to have regained his friendly attitude and she didn't want to upset the applecart again today.

Seeing as she had nothing to say, he sat gingerly down on the narrow deck, his legs extended, leaning on his arms. He eyed the far horizons.

'Sorry I was touchy at lunch,' Dominic said at long last, almost as if he were talking to himself. 'Marybeth died a long time ago, just before my first book was published. She was. . . she was as different from the women in my books as it is possible to get. Kind and gentle and very shy. Very sweet.' He was silent a while. 'Now the gals in my books are more like you, Lexy—self-sufficient, in charge of their lives. Going off on some adventure confident things will always come right, yet with an aura of femininity and innocence about them that attracts the hero.'

Lexy closed her eyes at the unexpected tribute. Did he really see her thus? Self-sufficient, feminine, innocent? If he only knew!

'You are restful and serene to be around.'

She permitted a brief smile to come to her lips, opening her eyes to see his gaze on her. 'I work at it,' she admitted. Worried as to where the conversation might lead, she quickly changed the subject. 'How long before we reach Bridgetown?'

He scanned the sky and sea before answering. 'Another four days, I figure.'

Four days. Lexy had enjoyed the hours spent thus far on the Marybeth. If things continued smoothly, perhaps the arrangement could continue while he wrote this book. Several months' work on the Marybeth would be lovely. She'd need to get some more books in Bridgetown, to keep herself busy while he worked. If they anchored while he wrote, she'd be able to swim each day as well. It would be an idyllic few months, more a vacation than a job. She hoped she could continue beyond Bridgetown.

They sat in companionable silence as the afternoon breeze

drove the sloop steadily northward to Barbados. Drowsily, Lexy felt relaxed and content.

Life was slow and peaceful on the sloop. She'd pull her weight, do her share, and be left alone to spend her time as she wanted while Dominic Frazer wrote his book. Her past life seemed to fade as her hopes for a bright future arose. Was her luck turning?

2

Lexy pulled a T-shirt over her swimsuit before starting dinner. While a swimsuit was entirely suitable for deck wear, she didn't feel it proper for cooking and eating. By many standards, she was still greatly under dressed, but the heat in the cabin made further clothing excessive. She was cooking chops in a pan on the propane stove when Dominic came down.

'I'll pile these papers up and we can eat on the table tonight,' he told her, gathering up the scattered sheets and stacking them into neat piles near the bulkhead.

'Fine. Where do we eat when you are full into writing?'

'Usually topside, if the weather's good. In the past we anchored near a small island and it's cooler on the deck after cooking and the general heat of the day. We'll lose the breeze through the portholes when we anchor.

He finished clearing the table and sat on the bench, watching her as she cooked. Lexy's brown legs were shapely, coming beneath the light blue T-shirt. She held her head high, as if trying to gain inches. Dominic smiled as he watched her, relaxed, content. She was a small thing, but with a huge determination. He was curious about her. What made her choose this kind of life?

'Lexy, do you worry about your reputation, traveling alone with me?' he asked suddenly. The thought had occurred to him before but it was one she may not have considered, the consequences of sailing for an extended period with an unmarried male. Standards and life-styles were rather casual in the West Indies, but even so, he was concerned lest she be hurt by any senseless chatter that might result from their sailing together.

She went still for a moment, shoulders oddly hunched as if fighting a sharp jab. Remain calm, she told herself; take a deep breath. Slowly she relaxed, answering in an odd voice, 'No, I don't worry about my reputation.'

'You needn't,' he continued. 'I loved my wife very much.' As if that explained everything.

Lexy sighed softly, a second dart of pain in her chest. Yes, that explained everything. He loved his dead wife and had found no one to take her place, to interest him, to tempt him. She would be very safe with him, unlike...

Not that it mattered; her sailing alone with him would do her reputation no harm, if he only knew.

The days passed quickly, almost too quickly. Lexy dipped again into the pile of books Dominic had on board, finding them light reading, a pleasant way to pass the hours while he worked. They split the night watch; during the day she kept an eye on the sails, the wind and their direction. The steady trade winds that plied the West Indies kept their daily speed constant, their adjustment of the sails to a minimum. Occasionally she sighted another boat on the horizon, and one morning one came within hailing distance and she exchanged waves with the several people on board. For the most part, however, the sea was theirs.

Lexy gazed longingly each hot afternoon at the inviting water, wishing she could dive beneath its surface, cool her hot body in the velvet warmth of the Caribbean. Maybe one day soon, if she stayed on, if she was hired for the whole cruise, then she would be able to take advantage of their anchorage and swim every day.

She let the book she was reading drop down, her eyes on the far horizon, her thoughts miles away. They'd sight Barbados tomorrow night or the following morning.

She knew already, on her part, she'd like to continue the association; she hesitated to term it a job, and the duties required were so few and far between. Imagining how they would deal at the anchorage, she felt she would have even less to do in the way of work; meals would be about all, and she had to fix herself something to eat anyway. Where was the work? Paid vacation more like it.

Lexy wondered how Dominic felt. She was surprised, when reviewing the last few days, at the little actual contact they'd had. Meals were the only times, really, and although they were pleasant encounters, they were not of long duration. Splitting the night watch as they did caused Lexy to retire early to get enough sleep before her shift. Dominic then slept, awakening in the morning ready to work. He continued to use the port bunk while Lexy had the wheel and she wondered if their docking in Bridgetown would necessitate his converting the sofa, or if he'd stay in town with his brother.

But maybe it wouldn't matter to her; maybe she would be looking for a new job.

While she'd learned little about Dominic Frazer's private life, she'd been told a great deal about his much-loved younger brother, Robin, and his recent marriage in Bridgetown. His leaving the Marybeth had been a blow to Dominic, but working for his new father-in-law in his marine insurance firm assured Robin of continued interaction with the ships and sea. Dominic had seen him only briefly since his marriage and was looking forward to visiting him while in Bridgetown.

Finishing the breakfast dishes the next morning, leaving them to drain on the small galley counter, Lexy went topside.

She picked up another book--one she'd read several years ago–
to reread today. If she stayed she'd buy several dozen new books
in Bridgetown to bring with her. She wondered briefly where she
would put them all, then remembered the port bunk wouldn't be
in use then. She'd use that as a bookcase.

'Ready to take over, sir,' she threw Dominic a saucy salute
and sank down near the wheel. 'Oh, you've lowered the jib,' she
noticed, looking up.

'Yes. I want to slow us up a little. The winds have been good
these last few days we've made excellent time. I don't want to
arrive in Bridgetown after dark. This should slow us down
enough to sight land tomorrow morning.'

'Aren't you going to work?' she asked, surprised to find him
comfortably ensconced and looking as if he were set for the
morning.

'Not today, Miss Slavedriver. I'm pretty well set now. I'm
taking today off.'

'I see,' she teased. 'And tomorrow, too, shocking waste of
time.'

He smiled back. 'Not at all, I'm thinking.'

She laughed at this, her dimple coming and going in her
cheek. They sat in companionable silence for a while, enjoying
the early morning warmth, the pleasant balmy air that hadn't yet
heated up to the humid torpor of the afternoon. The early
morning hours were the best in the West Indies.

'Tell me about yourself, Lexy,' Dominic invited lazily.

She looked around, startled at the question.

'What's to tell?' Her gaze swung out to sea. Darn, she had
hoped this would not come up. It hadn't before, why now?

'You tell me. I know you're quiet and self-sufficient. Most
women talk incessantly, or so it seems.' He mimicked in a high
falsetto, 'I adore sailing, I absolutely *love* the weather here, you

know I find your company *fascinating*, imagine little old me in company with a famous author.'

She chuckled appreciatively. 'That last one hit home, Dominic. I was thinking that very thing the other day, when you first told me. But I do hope I'm not a gusher.'

'No, you certainly aren't that, or much of a talker at all, come to think of it. I know by your accent that you're from England, not around here. I know your age because you told me, and you're an orphan. What else? Sisters or brothers?'

She was silent a long minute, staring out to sea. Now was her opportunity. He'd only know what she chose to tell him.

'No brothers or sisters. No one, just me, now. I was raised, as you suspected, in the West Country. Left England at eighteen for adventure.' She laughed mirthlessly. 'Some adventure. Oh, well, I've knocked around and here I am.'

'That's all? No husband, no boyfriend?'

She flushed again, slightly, avoiding Dominic's eyes. Shutting her mind down on the memories.

'Once, a long time ago, I thought I was in love,' she said very gently, so gently Dominic almost missed the words, but not the bitter voice. 'Never again,' she bit out.

Smiling wryly at this, he shook his head, she was still young. Plenty of time for some other man to catch her fancy. His curiosity was aroused, though. There was a story in those few words. Who had the man been and what had he done to make Lexy so bitter? At least the experience hadn't seemed to have warped her personality. She was open, friendly, candid.

Lexy was still staring at the distant horizon. She hated being reminded of the past. She hated it all. Her happy childhood only a cruel mockery of the promise her future had once held, bright and unending. She'd destroyed it, of course, and caused the change. She alone. Circumstances thereafter continued her on her new track, however much she tried to get off, to change back. It was impossible, she could never go back—and never change people's minds. It was the one unarguable fact she found over and over; people believed what they wanted. Explaining, excusing, nothing mattered—people believed the worst. And there was no escape. She'd tried, even thought she'd been successful once or twice, but in vain. The past always caught up with her.

She sighed; unaware of Dominic's watchful eye, unaware he had been studying her for the last few minutes, wondering at the bitter expression, at the sad look on her usually serene face.

'I'll go forward and lie in the sun a while,' she said, rising and holding out the book. 'I want to reread this, a competitor of yours.' It was an early Alistair MacLean adventure.

Dominic watched her as she went to the bow, then settled himself more comfortably to enjoy the breeze and balmy air. He wasn't through finding out more about his new crew woman, but for now he'd let it go. But he wondered.

'Lexy, time for lunch. I'm hungry even if you aren't,' he called several hours later.

She looked up from her absorption in her book, the earlier discussion forgotten. 'Okay, I'll get it.' She rose lithely and went below.

Dominic rechecked the compass, the sails, adjusted and lashed the wheel and followed. He settled in his bench, his cut-offs baring long brown legs, his chest and shoulders tanned almost as dark as his face.

Lexy glanced over and met his eyes. Flushing slightly she turned back to her work, unexpectedly aware of his presence, his maleness. She swallowed hard, willing her heart rate to slow down. 'I'm surprised at your dark tan,' she said into the suddenly tense silence. 'I thought blue- eyed people didn't tan so darkly.' She placed their plates on the cleared patch on the table and sat opposite him, very conscious of his nearness.

'Been in the sun most of my life. I think my skin has just been baked too long.' He smiled and began eating.

During lunch he broached the subject of her remaining, saying bluntly and without small talk, 'So far things have gone well. I want you to stay on, how do you feel about it?' His expression was serious, his bright blue eyes awaiting her answer.

She considered it for a moment. If he'd asked her yesterday, she'd have jumped at a yes. Now, after this morning, she wasn't as sure. Would he ask more disturbing questions, bring up the past she wanted buried? They had gotten along so well, except for the awkward time this morning and when she'd found out about his wife. She weighed it up and gave him a slow nod.

'Thank you for the offer. I'd like to stay on.'

'You're not going to get bored, now, are you?' he asked sharply. 'I might go days on end without stopping except for meals and sleep.'

'I won't if I can pick up some more books in Bridgetown. If I get a few dozen I can stow them on the port bunk, and read and swim while you're busy. I can amuse myself.' She was quietly confident on that score. 'We will anchor some times, won't we. I'd really love a swim.'

He nodded. 'I usually stay out a month or so at a time, can't carry enough food and water for much beyond that. I don't always come in to Bridgetown to restock, however— any island with the supplies that's close will do. It'll take three or four months at best; I write it out, then polish and trim the draft. It depends, sometimes it goes fast.' He shrugged.

She nodded. 'Can I use your snorkeling equipment when we're at anchor?'

'I assume you know how?'

'Yes, I did a lot with Miles, scuba diving too, but you don't have scuba equipment.'

'No, but if we go to my aunt's place when I surface for a break, we can do some diving. There's equipment at her place.'

'Where's that?'

'A little island in the Grenadines. I often combine re-stocking with a duty visit. She's my father's eldest sister, a bit of a character, but worth visiting briefly several times a year. Any more and I'd be driven to murder, I think. She has what's called a mind of her own, and doesn't mind telling everyone around her exactly what she thinks on any subject, and in a voice loud enough to wake the dead.'

'Sounds delightful,' Lexy smiled, trying to envision an old lady trying to get the best of this nephew of hers. He seemed too confident, too assured.

'We'll see what you think after you meet her,' he smiled back, his tone teasing.

'How long will we be in Barbados?' Lexy asked, still conscious a salary hadn't been mentioned, and wondering how to introduce the subject.

Two or three days. I'm staying at Robin's, and you'd better come too. I don't want you staying at the marina alone.'

'Oh, no,' she exclaimed involuntarily. He looked up at this, puzzled. 'I'd rather be on my own, if it is just the same to you,' she tried to explain.

'I don't think it's wise for you to be alone on the boat in harbor,' he repeated.

'I'll be fine, really.'

'I'd like you to meet Robin and Sarah.'

'Maybe,' she temporized. 'But all I have to wear are jeans and shorts. I don't have any dresses or anything, so will probably give it a miss this time.' There, that excuse should be good enough.

'Buy a dress,' he threw back at her.

Lexy faced him squarely, her eyes grave and serious, seemingly too large for her face. 'Dominic, everything I own is in the box and duffel bag I brought on board. I have nothing in them I don't need, nor any extra room for something like a dress that I might wear one time to meet your brother, then find superfluous. I don't want to buy something so unnecessary to me.'

'But surely when you go out or something. . .'

She shook her head. 'I don't go out,' she stated flatly. 'Please don't pursue the subject, it's embarrassing for me.' She fiddled with her napkin, her head down bent.

Dominic's lips tightened, but he kept his peace. If he wondered why she carried everything she owned with her, and why she didn't go out, he wouldn't let his curiosity show. He let the subject drop. But it was another frustrating fact that he couldn't understand about her.

Lexy turned her beer bottle around and around, worried about her salary, wondering again how to bring up the subject. Especially after snubbing him. She didn't know how, but if she lost courage now she might never ask, might go along for nothing but her room and board, which was payment of a sort, of course. Maybe even sufficient payment for her services. Darn, she didn't know what to do.

'If you don't go, you don't go,' he said. She looked up almost forgetting what they had been discussing. 'However, I'd like you to do the food shopping while we're in port. I'll give you the money tomorrow. If you want to make a list, or whatever, plan on at least four weeks at sea. I don't like a lot of sweets, but suit yourself, too, in planning the supplies. I usually shop at a couple of places near the pier that deliver. I'll get you their addresses in the morning. Pay you then as well,' he finished coolly.

'Pay me?' she squeaked, she didn't have to bring it up after all.

'Your salary,' he explained with exaggerated patience.

'But you never mentioned salary in Santa Inez. I did wonder,' she admitted.

'You should've said something,' he sounded impatient. 'Of course I pay a salary.'

'I was afraid to bring it up.'

'Afraid to? Why?' he thundered, astonished.

'Well, in Santa Inez because I didn't want to jeopardize my transportation to Barbados if room and board was all the pay. Then, just a minute ago, I thought you might be annoyed with me and ...' she trailed off, shrugging her shoulders expressively.

'Not annoyed, disappointed perhaps that you won't be meeting Robin and Sarah, but that has nothing to do with the job at hand.'

'You must admit that I don't do a lot for a salary. Fix the meals, and you've done most of the lunches.'

'Ah, but I'm paying for your expertise.'

'My expertise? In cooking?'

'No, in your knowledge of sailing. In a storm or other difficult situation, I need someone to back me up, someone who knows what they are about, who has a fair knowledge of sailing. I also require someone who's pleasant and available for conversation when I want them but who can keep quiet and out of my way when I don't want company. So, you fit the bill, and with a bonus.'

'A bonus?'

He smiled at her, a twinkle in his eye, 'You're pretty, too.'

Lexy's heart leaped at his words, as a warm glow filled her. He wanted her to stay. They would sail together for a time, getting to know each other better, exploring a new friendship, and maybe. . . She shook her head faintly, one thing at a time. She had the job!

'Thank you, kind sir,' she inclined her head at his compliment, then said cheekily, 'is that the best you can do, a writer, a person who has a way with words, just pretty?'

He laughed at her: 'Yep, that's all, so don't go fishing for more.'

3

They tied up at a pier at a private marina near the Bridgetown harbor early the following afternoon. From early dawn they'd seen signs that they were approaching civilization. A few boats scattered here and there on the horizon were the first indications, their number swelling as Lexy and Dominic drew closer to the island. Trash and bottles and cans floated by, marring the pristine beauty of the turquoise sea—a sure sign of modern man. By noon the dark shape of Barbados appeared on the horizon, growing larger each minute as the sails took as much wind as Dominic could coax and sent the boat along at a spanking clip.

Lexy stayed on deck after lunch, dressed decorously in shorts and a sleeveless top. She'd been to Bridgetown before, but was not immune to the excitement of a return trip. She kept an eye out for the towers and buildings she would recognize.

They skimmed by the commercial harbor where pleasure boats, fishing crafts and cruise ships filled the waters, giving a confused, chaotic appearance. Lexy watched anxiously, certain one ship would collide with another. None did, however, to her relief.

'Drop the jib.' Dominic called. 'Furl it then drop the mainsail.'

She glanced over her shoulder as she moved to obey the order. The throb of the auxiliary engine giving the answer of why he no longer wanted the sails. She complied swiftly, having only a little difficulty with the mainsail. When both were furled, covered and snapped into place she joined him at the helm, still eagerly watching the movement and antics in the harbor.

'Too crowded to use sails?' she asked as she stood by Dominic at the helm.

'Yes. See the pink house on the bay over there.' He pointed it out to her. 'We head for that. Below it is the marina I use when here. It's only about five minutes from town by taxi.'

She watched, and admired, the way he handled the forty-foot-long sloop in the busy waterways. His hands were firm on the wheel, in command. Constantly he scanned the water, trying to anticipate the directions the other boats might make, watching for the crazy holiday-maker who didn't know what he was doing and shouldn't have been let out on the water in the first place.

Lexy recognized some of the buildings on the shore now. The big high-rise American-owned hotel, and the department store near the main harbor. She smiled. She might not be able to do much this afternoon, but she'd have all day tomorrow to herself. She'd revisit old sites, treat herself to a real old-fashioned tea, maybe visit a hairdresser and have her hair trimmed.

When they were securely tied, Dominic stood and stretched.

'It'll feel odd at first on land. Want to get your passport, Lexy? I'll see to the landing formalities.'

He turned to give a final check on the wheel and palmed the engine key and so missed the startled look on her face. She had not anticipated this. Of course they had to go through immigrations and customs.

'I'll come along,' she said. With any luck, they'd have different lanes and he'd never see her passport.

'You can if you want. Bring it along. They're casual here, the formalities won't take but a minute.' He went to the cabin and got his from the drawer near the table, returning to the deck. Lexy was still standing where he had left her, anxiously looking towards shore.

'Come on,' he said impatiently.

Lexy went to get her blue passport with the fancy gold insignia. Clasping it in her hand, she followed him down the pier, oblivious to the boats on either side, to the people they passed. Worried only what would happen if Dominic saw the name on the passport.

Following closely behind Dominic, lost in thought, she bumped into him when he stopped to open the door to the marina office. He turned around and gripped her upper arm, pulling her gently around before him. 'Not got your land legs yet?' he murmured, opening the door so she could precede him.

She murmured something, her heart racing at his touch. She needed to focus, not imagine some reaction to his touch.

A low center counter bisected the office. A young woman in a coral sundress was seated at one end. Behind her were several desks, cluttered with papers and forms. There was a young man holding a phone against his ear, an expression of acute boredom on his face.

'May I help you?' the woman asked with a friendly smile.

'I hope so, Jim Travers out?' Dominic replied.

'Yes, for the rest of the day. Can I do anything?'

'I'm Dominic Frazer. I've just tied up to your visitors' pier and want to stay a few days.'

Lexy's mind wandered as Dominic explained to the mooring official. She looked out of the large windows, her eyes then drawn to the bored young man. Idly, she wondered to whom he was listening and what they were saying. She looked back at Dominic. He was obviously making a terrific impression on the woman. She was practically falling over herself in an attempt to do as much for him as she could. Lexy smiled, wondering if Dominic would classify her as a 'gusher'. Then a tinge of remorse smote her. The woman was young and looked nice. She was also looking at Lexy now.

'Now your passport and we'll be all set,' she was saying.

Lexy blinked and fatalistically handed it over, her eyes on the clerk, watching her open it briefly, check the picture then copy down the number. A quick glance at Dominic showed he wasn't at all interested in the proceedings, but was watching a man on the dock.

'Thank you, Miss Kent—'

'Call me Lexy,' she said hurriedly, too hurriedly. Dominic's puzzled look swiveled to her face. 'It's my nickname,' she said lamely.

The clerk found nothing amiss in this, only smiled again and nodded. 'Hope your stay here is pleasant.'

Dominic remained silent as they went outside, but Lexy knew he was looking at her in perplexity once or twice.

'Here's a phone.' Dominic paused at the covered phone booth at the entrance to the pier. 'I want to let Robin know I'm here. Want to wait, or go on back to the boat?'

'You don't have a cell phone?' she asked, surprised he still used the public landline.

'Where would I use one sailing? Besides, one of the reasons I write on the boat is to avoid interruptions," he said, fishing out some coins from his pocket.

'I'll go on, then. See you back at the boat. Or will you go directly to Robin's?'

'I'll be back for some clothes.' He began dropping coins in the slot.

Lexy nodded and sauntered slowly back down the pier, relieved immigration had gone so smoothly. It was much hotter tied to the dock than in the open, skimming the waves. The prevailing breeze was from the east and the landmass that was Barbados sheltered Bridgetown from the full cooling effect of the wind. She expected she'd just have to endure the heat until they set sail again in a few days.

She studied the other boats as she walked along, some inhabited, some secured tightly against the sun and weather, awaiting their owner's return. One large cabin cruiser was having a party, and one of the men called an invitation to her to join them, but she smiled and refused. She could hear his entreaty for several yards beyond the boat. Foolish, probably drunk already, she thought.

It was hot! She eased the shirt away from her body, fanning a little, trying to create a breeze. Maybe she'd book into a nearby, cheap hotel for the night. Anything would do, as long as it had air-conditioning. The cabin would be stifling with no air stirring. When Dominic left, she would ask that nice clerk in the office if she could recommend a good place close by. She didn't want to venture into town if she could help it.

'All set?' she asked brightly when Dominic joined her a few minutes later.

'Yes.' He gave her a warm smile. 'Come with me,' he coaxed. 'You'll enjoy meeting Robin and his wife.'

She was tempted, very tempted.

'Come on, say yes, if only for tonight,' he tried again, as if seeing she was weakening. 'Robin's place is air- conditioned,' he threw out slyly.

She burst out laughing. 'Sold! I was just thinking of an air-conditioned hotel room, it's hot here.'

'That's an understatement. I'm glad you changed your mind. Get a few things, bring a bathing suit, they have a nice pool, too.'

Rather excited for the first time in a long while, Lexy

gathered a change of clothes, sleepwear and her bathing suit. She stuffed it all into her capacious denim bag, slung it on her shoulder, and was ready.

She was quiet on the taxi ride to the Frazer's home, watching the once familiar sights of Bridgetown; the lovely colorful flowers that flourished in the gardens, the bright primary colors in the clothes worn by natives and tourists alike. Even the houses themselves were dressed up by English standards. Pinks, yellows and blues looked festive and foreign. She gazed her fill, enjoying the experience. Tomorrow she'd head for town for all the activity. Today she'd enjoy the quiet residential area.

They drew up before a dazzling white villa, a low wall encircling and enclosing the garden. Riotous red-and- pink geraniums grew profusely, contrasting with the stark whiteness of the stucco. Ornate black wrought-iron grills covered the windows. The villa sat on a small rise, overlooking the sea.

Before Dominic could pay the cab driver, the front door flew open and a young woman dashed out and over to him, hugging his arm, reaching up to give him a kiss on the cheek. Lexy stood back and watched, bemused.

'Oh, it's so good to see you, Dom; we've been waiting ages! Honestly, we thought you'd never come. Won't Robin be delighted when he gets home and finds you're here? I didn't call him to tell him, what a fun surprise, don't you think he'll be surprised? I know he will! I can't wait to see his face.'

As she paused to draw breath, Dominic skillfully interrupted and introduced Lexy to his scatterbrained sister-in-law, Sarah. She was of average height, an inch or two taller than Lexy, with corn-colored hair in plaits. She welcomed Lexy, her smile warm and friendly, and she laughed at Dominic's description of her.

'Isn't he funny? But it's because he's a writer, you know, and they're so frightfully clever. Robin's not, thank God. He's a perfect lamb and I love him to pieces, but he's not a bit clever and doesn't make you feel stupid or silly or anything.' She shot a telling look to her brother-in-law, but did not pause. 'Come in now, come in. I know you're dead tired and want to freshen up. I don't want any napping now, though. You don't feel like a nap do you? No, good. Do take a shower if you like, or whatever. Would you prefer to swim, the pool's around the side.'

'Yes,' Dominic said firmly. 'Lexy has a swimsuit and I know is dying to cool off. Just show her where to change and I'll meet you ladies at the pool.' Dominic sketched a salute and disappeared down the hall.

'Good idea, I love to swim, too. I think the yellow bedroom is ready; you can have that one, Lexy. That's a pretty name, Lexy. Is it short for something?'

'Alexis.'

'Umm, nice. Here is your room. Towels and things in the bath across the hall. Come out when you are ready, see you then.' Sarah gave her brief directions to find the back yard and pool then bounded away.

Lexy closed the door with relief. She knew now where Dominic found his prototype of the gusher. Sarah seemed nice, but talked so rapidly and so incessantly. Oh, well, one would never feel an outsider in this house, her warm welcome had been sincere. Idly she wondered if Dominic had been clever and hurtful at Sarah's expense, but from the little she knew about him, he didn't seem the type, From his talk on the boat she thought him genuinely fond of his brother's wife, but she'd get a better feel for things when she had observed them together for longer. She wondered what Robin was like, not being clever and all. Suddenly she giggled—the evening should prove entertaining.

Lexy brought a large white bath towel with her to the pool,

unsure if there would be any towels there. She ventured on to the tiled patio and glanced around. Except for the large tubs of geraniums flanking the sparkling pool, and the lounge chairs drawn up near its edge, the place was empty. She paused for a moment, enjoying the fantastic panoramic view from the terrace, down the colorful countryside to the azure water. Off to the far right the town of Bridgetown could be seen, the white buildings gleaming and bright in the distance. There was still no sign of anyone from the house. Shrugging, Lexy dropped her towel on a chair and dived into the inviting water.

Bliss! She leisurely swam to the end before surfacing. Floating on her back she reveled in the almost sensual pleasure that the water gave. Her hot sticky skin was caressed with the balmy chlorinated water, cooling down now to the pleasant temperature of the pool.

A wave of water, almost submerging her, announced Dominic's arrival. She trod water, shaking the drops from her eyes, trying to glare at him, but too pleased to have any effect.

'Isn't it grand!' she called.

They swam together, trying out different strokes and racing once or twice. Finally, relaxing and floating, each reluctant to leave the coolness. They heard voices and looked over to see Sarah coming out, carrying a tray of drinks, and followed by a tall man in a swimsuit. He helped Sarah with the tray, and then took a flying leap into the pool, almost landing on Dominic. During the ensuing water fight, Lexy prudently removed herself from the pool and joined Sarah, tying a towel around her sarong-fashion.

Sarah was laughing. 'That's Robin, I supposed you guessed. He was surprised when he saw Dominic, that's why we took so long to get out here. They had to talk a while, then Robin still had to change. Would you like a drink? I brought lemonade.

Dominic said you liked lemonade. I hope it's not too sweet. I do hate sweet-sweet lemonade, but if it's too tart let me know—we can add sugar. Much easier to add sugar than try to get rid of it, don't you think?'

Sarah rambled on, only needing an occasional acknowledgment to keep going. Lexy sat back in her chair and watched the brothers fighting in the water, watched as they gave up and finally left the pool.

Robin Frazer was as large as his brother, rather better looking, though his eyes were not the remarkable blue of Dominic's. His hair, too, was different, lighter, not yet flecked with gray, nor worn so long. He greeted Lexy warmly, welcoming her to his home, inviting her to stay as long as Dominic did.

She smiled and replied politely to the warm invitation of the young Frazer's, but did not let herself become too caught up with them. Just in time, she reminded herself she must watch against relaxing her guard, must keep herself aloof from warm friendships, any commitments. They ended sooner or later, with hurt and pain. She replied politely, but reservedly. She must watch herself.

They grilled steaks out of doors and ate, still in their swimsuits. The talk was easy and fun. Lexy was amused to notice early on that Sarah was not as talkative with her husband around. She deferred to him on many subjects and hung on his every word when he spoke. Touched by her obvious devotion, Lexy cynically wondered how long it would last. Catching Dominic's eye on her, she looked away quickly, hoping he hadn't read her mind. She genuinely liked both Sarah and Robin and wished them many years of happy married life.

Lexy had no difficulty in keeping up her end of the conversation. She could easily converse on a number of topics, but skillfully avoided anything personal. When Sarah had asked some questions about England, Lexy passed it off as not having lived there for so long, she wouldn't have the best answer. In response to Sarah's puzzled expression, Dominic explained that Lexy was older than she looked and had left England a number of years ago.

Speculative glances were exchanged between the younger Frazer's, but nothing was said, no questions asked aloud to their guests. Lexy appeared not to notice, although she had. There was nothing between Dominic and her. The tentative friendship they had was a start, and if in time–

She wrenched her thoughts back to the conversation at hand, keeping them firmly under control the rest of the evening.

Dominic rode into Bridgetown with Robin the next morning. He was going to pick up some paper, a new printer and other necessary supplies for the next few months. He told Sarah he wouldn't be home for lunch, but some time in the early afternoon.

When he had gone, the two girls lingered over their coffee. Sarah was going into town herself later and was giving Lexy a ride in at that time.

'Robin and I discussed it last night,' she said when the men had departed. 'We are going to have a small party tonight, just a few friends and neighbors who know Dominic. Joey will want to come too; he's their cousin. Since the weather is so good, no rain tonight, we can have it outside. You'll like the people, Mary Hendricks is English too, so you can talk about home together and ...'

Lexy put her cup down and shook her head, awaiting a pause in Sarah's monologue to speak. 'I'm sorry, Sarah, but I won't be here tonight. I used to work here in Barbados and. . . and had planned to see some old friends again,' she lied, improvising rapidly. 'I'm not free tonight or tomorrow.'

'Oh, but you must come, Lexy. We especially wanted you to meet our friends.' Sarah was clearly disappointed.

'Thank you for asking me, I would like to, but I've made plans. It will be more fun without me. Everyone knowing everyone else and seeing Dominic again.'

'Yes,' doubtfully. 'Tomorrow night?'

'No, busy then, too. And we leave the next day,' Lexy said gently.

Sarah tried to persuade her to alter some of her plans, tried to persuade Lexy to stay a while longer with the Frazer's, but Lexy held steadfast to her resolve, and seethed with impatience to be off, to gain the anonymity of the city. To lose herself for two days, escaping meetings and questions and explanations. She wanted to be on her own for a while, to be able to relax her guard and enjoy her limited time in Bridgetown. Outwardly she remained calm, pleasant and firm to Sarah's persuasions, but inwardly, she screamed at every delay to departure.

At last, she stood before the large Cave Shepard department store on Broad Street, bidding her hostess farewell, thanking Sarah again for her kindnesses and hospitality. The car door slammed and Lexy was free. She looked around, conscious of the heat rising up from the pavement, reflected from the buildings. The slight breeze evident near Sarah's house was now blocked by the edifices between Lexy and the sea. It was still, sticky and hot; and would only get worse as the day progressed.

Lexy pushed open the doors of the Cave Shepard and entered the cool ground floor of the department store. The cold air chilled her damp skin, cooling her rapidly, uncomfortably. She moved briskly along the aisles, telling herself she would be fine in a few minutes. Idly she browsed through the lingerie counters and displays. She had plenty of money with her;

Dominic had paid her yesterday. She wouldn't spend it all, though; she never spent all her salary, always saving something against the times when she was out of work. She had been flat broke once, and never wanted to be in such straits again. Today she'd find a bank and trade in some of the money for traveler's checks. They were safe, available everywhere and negotiable everywhere. She didn't stay in one place long enough to have a bank account.

She found herself in the better dress department, and for a few minutes let her gaze wander over the lovely creations on display, even letting her imagination picture herself in one or two. Picturing herself dazzling Dominic, having him speechless with admiration. She shook her head, foolish dreams.

In the sportswear section she treated herself to a couple of new shirts and vainly to a pair of brief shorts, she knew her legs were good, and these showed them off to advantage. She hesitated over a bathing suit, but already owning three, she did not need another.

Her shopping completed for the morning, she slowly headed for the main door. She'd treat herself to a lavish lunch, with cream-filled pastries for dessert. Then she'd look for books. There would be plenty of time tomorrow to get the ship's supplies, fill the water tanks and unpack everything. She had nothing else to do to fill her time until they sailed.

She pushed the heavy door, the suffocating heat hitting her like a blow in the face. Whew, she stopped by the building to get her breath, it was awful after the coolness of the store.

'Going my way?' a familiar voice accosted her.

Lexy looked up to familiar blue eyes gazing down on her, and smiled.

'Hi, Dominic, I was going to lunch now, where are you going?'

'Lunch. Have it with me. Any place special?'

'I don't know many restaurant here in Bridgetown, but I want one that has cream-filled pastries for dessert,' she admitted with a smile. 'They're a weakness of mine.'

His smile almost stopped her breath, it was warm and friendly and a little more. 'I know just the place, honey, come with me.'

The casual endearment did strange things to Lexy's heart and she felt in that instance that she'd follow him anywhere as long as he smiled at her like that and called her honey.

They had a lovely lunch at a small teashop just a stone's throw from Broad Street. It was comfortably full, without being crowded and they were able to find a table near a window. For dessert Lexy had her large, rich, chocolate-covered éclair. She joyfully savored every mouthful causing Dominic's eyes to gleam in amusement. They were lingering over the last of their beverages when Dominic mentioned the party that evening.

'It's casual, you know, so jeans or shorts are appropriate,' he smiled.

Lexy licked her lips, suddenly dry. 'I won't be going,' she said in her soft voice. 'I already explained to Sarah. I —um—there are some old friends here and I'm spending the evening with them. Tomorrow, too,' she added quickly. She shrugged helplessly. 'I'm sorry. I did enjoy meeting Robin and Sarah. I think they're both delightful people.'

If Dominic regretted her missing the party, he made no sign. He murmured a brief, 'Sorry you'll miss it,' and closed the subject.

'What time are you meeting your friends, Lexy?' he asked as they prepared to leave the teashop.

'About—about five,' she stammered, surely the party would not begin before then.

'That leaves us the afternoon together. Would you like to see Sam Lord's castle, a sugar refinery, take a walk along the wharf?'

'Yes,' she said promptly. It sounded like a fun afternoon in his company, away from the boat, away from people who knew them. She'd get her books tomorrow. That would fill in the time the Frazer's thought she had committed to friends.

'Yes, what?' he asked.

'All of them, if we have time?'

Dominic sat back in his chair and chuckled. 'I don't know, we can try. What we miss, maybe your friends will take you to see.'

'Umm.' She was non-committal.

He paid the bill and hailed a cab. After a brief stop at the marina to drop off her purchases, they headed inland. Sam Lord's castle was a must-see for the tourists in Barbados. Sam Lord had been a pirate who had lured ships on to the rocks along Barbados' Atlantic coast, salvaging their cargo. He built himself a grand mansion overlooking the cliffs he used, and the workmanship was splendid. He'd had the money to import Italian craftsmen to complete the house and it was said he spared no expense to have the finest house in the Caribbean.

As they rode along the main highway from Bridgetown to the castle, Dominic explained that it had recently been purchased by an American hotel firm and they had discreetly added buildings nearby and turned the entire complex into an unusual and expensive resort.

'For only a small charge, however, the public can still view the Castle. The furnishings are the original, or replicas of the same. The view is fantastic,' Dominic said.

Lexy was eager to see the landmark. She had not taken the tour when she'd been on Barbados before.

After touring the complex, they headed back towards

Bridgetown. On the way, the road curved near a sugar refinery, which was open to the public.

Lexy was fascinated at the steps taken to transform the raw cane to molasses, then refined white and brown sugars. The large vats, the heat and the strong smells only added to the interest she found in the process. At the tour's end she bought a small sample pack, for a souvenir. A small reminder of a happy afternoon.

They waited in front of the refinery for a cab, standing in the shade of a palm tree. Dominic casually checked his watch.

'How late is it?' she asked reluctantly.

'After four. I'm afraid we'll have to give the wharf a miss, if you don't want to be late meeting your friends.'

Lexy's spirits dropped, though she pinned a bright smile on her face. The precious afternoon was going by faster than she thought. If only there were some way to stop the time, keep it still on these happy hours. She had enjoyed their time together. They'd discussed current events, authors, and music–finding a lot in common, a lot of mutual likes. She could feel the warmth in their relationship, a strong liking, not only on her part, but with Dominic, too.

She almost changed her mind about the party, almost told Dominic to heck with her imaginary friends, she'd return to Robin's with him. She was reluctant to let him go, reluctant to delay the growing awareness between them. But she must. It would only be for a day and a half, then they would be together for a month, only the two of them, alone on the Marybeth. When he wasn't working, they'd have loads of time to explore their feelings, have them grow. She smiled in anticipation. It should be a wonderful cruise.

The cab drew up.

'I'll take this cab out to Robin's after I drop you. Where to?'

'The Coral Reef,' she said, naming a large hotel in town.

They were silent in the cab, watching the scenes flash by, each aware that the time was fleeting, unable to stretch it out. When the hotel was in sight, Dominic turned to her.

'We'll sail the day after tomorrow. Will you have enough time to get everything?'

'Oh, yes, I plan to do a lot tomorrow, uh, while my friends are doing some business here. I plan to have everything delivered early Thursday morning, and I'll pack it away as it comes in. Should be ready before mid-morning.'

'Good, I think the tide turns at eleven, but we don't have to sail precisely at that time, we'll use the engine to take her out.'

The cab drew up to the hotel and stopped.

'Tell Robin and Sarah thanks again for me,' she muttered hurriedly, scrambling out.

Dominic followed her out. 'I'll see you, then, Thursday morning. Here's a spare key to the cabin, in case you arrive earlier than I.' He looked down at her a moment, then reached his hand to the back of her head, drawing her close and kissing her lightly on the mouth.

'See you Thursday, Lexy,' he said huskily, and was gone.

4

Dazed, Lexy watched the cab pull out and merge in the busy afternoon traffic. Gradually she became aware of the hustle and bustle of the pedestrians. Looking around she got her bearings and began walking up the street. She would stay in the Sundowner Hotel, on a small side street. She'd heard of it before, and it was close to Broad Street, quiet and cheap.

Lexy passed a restless night, thinking of Dominic Frazer and the impromptu party Sarah had arranged. She longed to be there, to be with him, even though she knew she had done the correct thing in refusing the invitation. She reminded herself she couldn't afford to mingle, be drawn into friendships. She had set her course, now she must stick to it.

Maybe things would be different this time. She and Dominic were already friends—maybe they would draw closer, come to trust each other, believe in each other. Then, she could tell Dominic. He would understand, he would believe her and then she'd be like other women, who fall in love, get married. The past would lose its power over her once and for all. She smiled at her daydreams. Longing for that moment to come. But she would bide her time in patience, and when the moment was right, tell him her story. Maybe when the cruise ended, maybe before.

The next day Lexy set out early to the addresses Dominic had provided. She'd spent the evening in the hotel planning meals that would be easy and quick to fix in the small galley, listing items she needed that would provide nutrition and have visual appeal. She had no difficulty in finding the stores, or in arranging to have the supplies delivered to the Marybeth. The establishments had dealt with Dominic before and appreciated his patronage.

That out of the way, Lexy went to find a bank and a bookshop.

At three o'clock a taxi deposited her at the foot of the pier. She unloaded her sacks of books, stacking them beside the ramp to the dock. Paying the driver, she lifted one bag and started down the pier. The party on the cruiser still seemed in full swing and Lexy wondered if it was the same one, or a new one started that day.

The sloop looked lonely and deserted when she came abreast of it. She hopped lightly aboard and put her bag by the cabin door. Taking the precious key from her denim shoulder bag, she unlocked the door, hooking it open.

It took her two more trips to bring all her purchases aboard. She was hot and sweating by that time, and thought longingly of the cool pool at the Frazer's. The cabin was like a furnace, hot and still. She dumped her books on the bunk and got a clean change of clothes from her drawers. She would organize her things when they left port—it was too hot now and she wasn't staying long enough to open all the portholes and try to cool the cabin down.

She up-ended her bags of books, choosing a mystery to take back to the hotel. She scattered her new library about, pleased with her selections and anxious to get started on reading them all. Mysteries, biographies, adventure stories, one or two non-fiction ones on sailing and tropical fish, one on poetry. She picked the last one up and smiled jeeringly at herself. 'Getting soft in your old age, girl.' She tossed it back and pulled the door closed.

Soon she was on her way back to the Sundowner. She toyed briefly with the idea of calling Dominic and saying her friends had left earlier than expected, but she'd feel too foolish. Tomorrow would come soon enough.

Lexy was up early the next morning. After a quick breakfast she paid her bill and caught a cab for the marina. When she paid off the driver she noticed a small bakery further along the road. With a happy smile she walked down the pier. Later, when the stores had arrived and been put away, she would dash over to the bakery and get some cream cakes and fruit tarts for the trip. They would be fine for a day or two, a last taste of city life.

It was still early, not yet eight, when Lexy opened the cabin door. Dominic had not arrived, so she set to work quickly. She was anxious to impress him with her dedication and determination. She opened the portholes, catching a little of the still cool morning breeze, blowing some of the staleness from the ship. She washed down the galley and sitting areas, and took all the old supplies from the storage bins. The goods arriving this morning would go in first, leaving these older tins and boxes to be put back in on top.

Right at nine the delivery boy hailed the sloop. Between them, all stores were loaded and put away before ten. Lexy thanked him for his help, giving him a generous tip. She danced a little step with glee. Things were going so well. Now, to go for the cakes and she would be ready when Dominic arrived.

'Good morning, Lexy.' Dominic was framed in the doorway, having boarded so quietly she had not heard him.

'Good morning, Dominic.' She stopped, bereft of further words, her heart tripping in her chest. He looked so familiar, so dear. She smiled shyly, glad to see him.

He swung casually into the cabin, a box of paper on one hand, the new printer in his other. Putting both on the table he scanned the cabin.

'Food not come yet?' he asked.

'Oh, yes, all put away. I told them to deliver early and they complied. I think I have everything. I only want to dash over to the bakery for a couple of cakes, and I'll be ready.'

'Good. Plenty of time, though. My cousin brought me over and I've still got some things in his car. Come on, I'll walk with you back up the pier.'

He helped her on to the dock, falling in with her smaller steps as they headed to shore.

'How did you find your friends? Did you get to go to the wharf?' he asked.

'Uh, they were fine. Actually we were too busy catching up on news and all to go about much. Next time, maybe. How was the party?'

'I enjoyed it.' He glinted a smile down to her. 'I could have enjoyed it more.'

Lexy felt her heart swell with happiness. What a nice thing to say.

They parted at the shore, Lexy for the bakery, now opened, and Dominic for the city parking lot.

'See you soon, we'll be shoving off in a little while, I've already cleared it with the marina.'

'Fine,' she smiled back, 'I won't be long.'

She walked slowly to the bakery, savoring the pleasant morning. Being by the sea, it was cooler than the town, the air circulated and moved, affording the illusion of coolness. She entered the shop, spending some fifteen minutes selecting cakes and tarts for their first nights out. The lady behind the counter was a friendly soul and very interested to learn of Lexy's job and destination.

'Wish I had something with a paid vacation at the end of it,' she declared as she put the cakes carefully into a pink cardboard box. 'Course I can get in a sail and a bit of a swim here, so it's not all bad,' she said cheerily.

Lexy walked back, bubbling with happiness. Soon they would be on their way, leaving the heat and bother of town life behind for several weeks. Days of sun and swimming, reading and generally enjoying life. Days with just herself and Dominic.

As she reached the sloop she could hear the murmur of voices from within. Dominic's cousin had evidently waited to meet her. She grinned, boarding the boat as quietly as Dominic had earlier.

She started down the steep steps into the cabin, gaily dangling the pink bakery box.

'I got us some lovely cakes for dessert, two cream ones!' she said smiling across the cabin at Dominic, he and his cousin seated at the table, Dominic facing aft, towards her.

At the sound of her voice Dominic's cousin turned, a sardonic grin covering his face at the sight of her.

'Well, well, well. Sexy Lexy. I wondered if it were you.' A malicious smile covered the man's face. His hair was dark, growing thick and long, his clothes were tight fitting and colorful, his sardonic expression masking his otherwise pleasant features.

Lexy's complexion paled as much as it could beneath her deep tan, her eyes widened in shocked disbelief.

'Joey Compton,' she whispered, darting a nervous glance at Dominic, reluctantly returning her eyes back to the other man. She felt sick, as if someone had punched her in the stomach. She swallowed hard. Joey Compton was the last person she had expected to see today or had ever wanted to see again.

She moved slowly across the cabin, carefully placing the

pink bakery box on the small counter, her mind spinning frantically. Reluctantly she turned back to face the two men, leaning against the sink's edge, depending upon it to keep her upright, her legs as weak as jelly, a sick feeling spreading in her stomach.

Dominic looked puzzled. 'You two know each other?' he asked. He was startled by Joey's greeting to Lexy.

Lexy's eyes pleaded with Joey Compton, but he sneered at her, raking her slight figure as she stood there before them. 'Sure I know her, have known her for years. Tried to get her to live with me once,' he inclined his head, mocking her. 'But I didn't have enough money for Sexy Lexy, huh, sweetheart?'

She was shaking her head from side to side, her eyes held by Joey's. 'No,' she spoke in a hoarse voice. 'No, Joey, don't do this.'

'What do you mean, Joe?' Dominic bit out, his eyes hard on his cousin.

'Miss Lexy here is what was known in the good old days as a high-price courtesan.'

'That's not true, that's not true!' she protested, her tongue licking her lips. Why did Joe have to show up now, just when she had a chance of things improving, a chance for some happiness!

'She lived with Miles Jackson for a number of years, till he tired of her and decided to marry a respectable girl. He passed her along to Tom Bullocks. After six months or so Tom was killed. That's when I made my offer, but she turned me down for some guy named Benson.' Joey tossed off the information, his eyes compelling, forcing Lexy to watch him.

'Bateson,' she corrected involuntarily, 'and it's not true, Joey, so don't keep talking. You don't know anything.'

'Oh, but it is true, sweets,' he sneered, leaning on the table, snaring her with his narrowed eyes, reveling in her distress, in the rigid attention of his cousin. 'Amelia Jackson told me all about you, she almost didn't marry Miles because of you. What about your escapade in merry old England?'

'Stop it, Joey, just stop.' She looked at Dominic, her face reflecting her distress, hurt and bewilderment showing in her large gray eyes. Surely Dominic would stand her friend.

Dominic sat as if carved from stone, his eyes narrowed and assessing. He studied her for a moment as if he had never seen her, then turned to Joey.

'What escapade in England?'

'No,' she protested, tears welling in her eyes, spilling down her cheeks. 'Please!' Lexy's hands came up and pressed on the pain in her chest. Why was he doing this to her? For revenge because she had refused to sleep with him? That had happened ages ago. Why wouldn't he stop? He was ruining everything.

'She was sleeping around with some married guy in England. When her family couldn't get her to stop, they cut her off and turned her out without a penny.'

Dominic's cold blue eyes swiveled to Lexy, his teeth clenched, his hand a hard fist on the table. 'Is any of this true?'

She shook her head to clear the pain, she could not see him clearly, only swimmingly through her tears. 'It's not like Joey says.' Her voice was ragged; she seemed to draw into herself, as if to ward off a blow.

'No good, babe,' Joey said breezily. 'Can't expect cousin Dominic, who has always been so true to his first love, to forgive so much in a tramp like you. I'm not as picky, but even I wouldn't want such shop-worn goods now. A fling is one thing, but Sarah intimated marriage last night, and that would never, never do. Not for our family.'

Lexy drew a shaky breath. She flicked a glance at Dominic. Studying his hands, he neither looked at her nor his cousin, his face closed, his eyes shuttered. She looked back at Joey Compton, sitting back now, his eyes slyly triumphant.

Dominic did not look up.

With a small sound, Lexy flung herself towards the haven of the small forward cabin. She closed the door, flinging herself on her bunk, curling up into a small ball, the tears streaming from her eyes, wetting her face, soaking her pillow. The ragged pain tearing at her breast.

When would it end? Was she to be punished forever and ever for some silly mistakes when she was a teenager? It had been eight years since her one slip. Eight years of loneliness, uncertainty, fear. Was she never able to escape the consequences of her girlhood folly? It had been a defiant childish gesture. Would she never be free of it?

It was cruel to have two such nice, happy days as these last had been, only to have the happiness snatch away and Joey's attack plunge her back into despair. She'd planned to tell Dominic. She could have explained it away, not like Joey had, so sordid and cheap, but showing it as a youthful folly. Given time, she would have told him herself.

She buried her face in the pillow, drying her tears, fighting to get herself under control again, fighting to ease the pain, ease her sense of loss. She'd have to leave. Pack her things and get off the boat.

Endless moments passed. Finally, she took a deep breath and lay back staring dully at the ceiling. Time to move. She would repack her duffel bag, re-tie her box of books. Sadly she turned her head to all the new books she'd bought. She wouldn't be able to carry all that along as well, and she had so wanted to read them. The tears welled again. Maybe with her next job.

She'd moved from job to job in the last eight years, all because of her hated reputation. Just when she would think herself safe and secure, a proposition would come. Men like Joey Compton who, if they thought she'd had slept with one man, saw no reason why she would refuse them. That awful Phil Bateson had tried. Joey had been most persistent, even offering to have her move in with him as he had said. Even Mrs. Culver's awful husband had tried. When she'd refused every one, they all got nasty, always after her for refusing them, making her life impossible with accidental meetings, quick, snatched kisses, until she'd up and leave. Not even getting a reference from Phil Bateson. It was unfair, so unfair.

She sighed. Well, that was that. She'd find another job here in Bridgetown. One, she needed to make sure would make it unlikely to run into anyone who knew her. It was a fair-sized city; she should be able to manage it.

Wearily she sat up, time to pack. Her eyes welled with tears again. She had so looked forward to sailing with him; looked forward to the promise that trip had held for them. Now it was gone. She brushed a tear away impatiently and set to work.

Her books repacked, she pulled out her duffel bag and opened the drawer, stumbling back as the ship lurched. Something was wrong. Something . . . she cocked her head. The engine. The boat's engine was running, its throbbing reverberating along the planking. She looked out of the porthole, the dock was slipping away. They were moving. They were leaving!

Lexy scrambled to her feet, threw open her door and stumbled into the cabin. It was deserted. She continued aft, bursting up on the deck. Dominic was at the helm, calmly maneuvering the sloop out, turning her bow seaward.

'Dominic, stop. I have to get off,' she cried, stumbling over to him. He regarded her coolly, disdainfully.

'You got your cakes, Miss Kent, what else do you need?' he

asked in that hard, cold tone he had used once before, just a short time ago, in the cabin.

'I ... I have to get off,' she repeated uncertainly, looking at him through her tear-blotched eyes, red-rimmed and swollen. 'Don't I?' A small spark of hope burgeoning in her. Maybe he believed in her, maybe he would stand by her, discount what Joey had said and listen to her explanation.

'I told you we sailed at eleven.'

He looked out to sea, ignoring her.

'But that. . . that was before Joey said all those awful things. You can't want me to sail with you now. Do you?' Still that hope.

'To be forewarned is to be forearmed, Miss Kent. I shan't permit any of your blandishments to beguile me into thinking you're the sweet, innocent young thing you obviously are not. However, if I do not sail with you, I have to find a replacement, and that could take days, several days. Time I don't have. I do have a schedule to meet and want to stick to it.'

'But I don't want to go, not with you thinking those awful things about me,' she protested.

'I asked you if any of it were true,' he looked down on her, his eyes searching.

'A grain only. Not like Joey said,' she tried to explain. 'If you'll let me explain, you'll see it is not as bad as it sounds.'

'What about England?' he snapped, his eyes narrowed and hard.

She dropped her eyes, 'That was partly true. My grandfather disowned me. Sent me away from home, but–'

'Your grandfather? I thought you had no family?'

She made no reply, licking her lips, eyes still on the decking, color rising in her cheeks.

'Go get your passport,' he said unexpectedly.

She did look up at this. 'My passport?'

'I want to see it. You've probably lied about your age, too.'

'No, I haven't,' she said. 'Truly.'

'Let me see.'

'You don't need to see it,' she said, sick again. She pressed her churning stomach.

Dominic latched the wheel with an angry movement and strode below, Lexy following him frantically.

'No, Dominic, please . . .' She was too late.

Upending her bag on her bunk, he selected the blue passport and opened it.

'Alexandra Kentfield,' he read, 'Larchmont Tower, Brayford, Dorset, England. Damn! Your name isn't even your own,' he said in disgust. 'You are nothing but a cheap lying tramp. Joey was right, damn him.'

'No, please, I can explain. I had planned to,' she said desperately, frantic for him to listen to her.

He stared at her for a moment, assessing her, weighing things in his mind. His face hard, unyielding, unforgiving. Dispassionately, he replied,

'Joey explained everything most adequately, thank you. I don't want the subject raised again. Your past life has no interest for me, no bearing on the job at hand. I trust Miles Jackson's letter is reasonably accurate about your experience and expertise. Considering the circumstances I wouldn't be surprised if it exaggerated some things a little, but I have seen that you do know something about sailing.'

'But Dominic . . .'

He raised his hand, his face suffused with anger, 'I assume you need a job, if you want the one going on this ship, you will do as I say. There will be no explanations from you, I don't need any. I don't want to discuss the matter again, is that clear?'

'Yes, but. . .'

'No, Miss Kent. . . Kentfield, damn, even your name's a lie.'

'More of a contraction,' she offered, biting her lip at his anger. 'Please . . .'

'How many people here in the Indies know your real name?'

'No one, I have always used Alexis Kent since I left England. I thought–'

'Then you can continue doing so, and leave it at that. I think I convinced Joey not to say anything further to anyone else, like Sarah or Robin. They liked you.' He sounded incredulous.

'Well, so did you until Joey came,' she replied smartly.

'Before I knew the facts,' he said in that hard, cold voice. 'You just do your job, and we will get on fine. I'll take her out. I'll call you when it's time to haul up the sails.' It was dismissal, clear and cold. He left the cabin and regained the helm.

Lexy held her head high as he left, cut to the quick he wouldn't listen to her, but refusing to show it. She sank slowly to her bunk, watching their progress through the portholes with dull, pain-filled eyes. She shook her head in confusion. Why was it everyone was so quick to believe somebody else? Why wouldn't they listen to her? Why not believe what she had to say? It happened over and over. She'd tried. On several occasions she'd told the truth, to no avail. No one believed her.

Dominic would not listen, preferring to believe Joey Compton.

Her grandfather had not believed her, nor Amelia Jackson, nor Phil Bateson.

She drew a shaky breath. Miles had believed her. Had met her and as a stranger believed her because of her truthful eyes. She sniffed, so much for truthful eyes with Dominic Frazer. She gazed out of her porthole as Bridgetown slid slowly by, seeing none of it, her thoughts turned inward.

They cleared the harbor, leaving the noise, the trash floating on the water and the diesel fumes hanging in the air, behind, gaining the clean open sea. At the wheel, the stern, determined man; below decks, a forlorn woman.

'Lexy. Hoist the mainsail,' he called when they had gained the open water.

She came slowly and moved to obey his order. Methodically, and without much thought, she unsnapped the canvas and hauled on the halyard. Dominic locked the wheel and moved to help, careful to avoid any physical contact with her. The sail bellowed, filled with wind, the boom swinging out to the proper angle. The boat leapt forward.

'Jib now,' Dominic said, returning to the helm.

That was one Lexy could manage on her own, and she did. When the sail was in place, she looked thoughtfully back at the boat's owner. He would probably work her harder now than before, but she would still find it easygoing. If he wanted it strictly impersonal, well, she would be happy to comply. From now on Mr. Frazer would get exactly what he paid for and not a smile or friendly word more. She faltered a moment as the pain tore across her again—he wouldn't even give her the opportunity to tell her side of it. He had judged and condemned without giving her a fair hearing. Well, no matter, she was back where she had been a week ago. She'd lived through worse and survived. She'd live through this.

It had been a mistake on her part to lower her guard at all, to hope, to dream foolish things. Her name was unusual enough that Joey had suspected, immediately upon hearing it, who she was. He had taken full advantage of that knowledge for a long-awaited revenge. She shook her head in remembrance of that awful weekend. She'd known Joey casually for several months, having met him through Amelia Jackson when she worked for Miles. Lexy remembered even now her surprise when Joey had invited her to go to that weekend party up in the hills above Bridgetown. Hesitantly, she had accepted. It wasn't long after Tom Bullocks' tragic death and she was still somewhat at a loss. The diversion might focus her attention elsewhere, she'd thought, might even be some fun.

The weekend had been a nightmare from start to finish. Beginning with Joey's veiled insinuations in the car on the way up; through his drinking heavily upon arrival, culminating with the awful scene in the lounge when Joey casually mentioned she was to share his room as part of the weekend. When she declined as gracefully as she could, Joey told her he knew that she had been living with Miles and Tom and that he was as good as either of them, and she could do a lot worse. Lexy had been stunned at his comment, shocked at what he thought. Was that what everyone thought—the same vile ideas Joey had of her living with Miles and with Tom?

Joey refused to hear her denials, of her attempted explanations. He grew more and more demanding, more obnoxious with each moment, oblivious to the couples that began drifting in drawn by Joey's loud voice.

Lexy had been unable to muster a defense. She hated scenes, felt sick and shaky, her mind would go blank, unable to think coherently. All she wanted was to escape.

That had been the final straw for Joey, when she, unable to endure any more, had walked out on him, in front of all his friends. She'd heard later that he had been the butt of many jokes from his friends for a long time after, and it was no wonder that he had wanted revenge.

She had felt a twinge of guilt from that trip. Perhaps by accepting the invitation she had led Joey on, given him reason to suspect she was that type of woman. Still, he should have accepted her refusal, not made such a big scene. She bit her lip.

Another person would have maintained harmonious relations, not ended the event so scandalously. But that wasn't the way it had turned out, and he had paid her out fine for any humiliation he had suffered by his friends.

She sighed deeply. Lexy so wished he hadn't come, wished— She raised her chin. She'd count it another lesson learned. No more friendships, no more relaxing her guard, no more foolish dreams. She'd make her way alone. It was the safe choice.

Supper was a strained affair. Dominic neither looked at her nor spoke from the time the first plate was set before him, until his coffee was placed at his side. Lexy, not risking a snub, refused to offer a word. She took pains to cook a good meal, put it before him and tried to ignore his presence, to no avail. She refused to let herself look at him, but was aware of his every move. She was gratified with the way he ate everything, but would have liked some verbal praise. Still, she didn't ask, not wanting to hear his cold cutting tone directed towards her again.

He left for the deck immediately after dinner, leaving Lexy in solitude to clear the table and clean the dishes. She reflected bitterly how times had changed. Their last night before Bridgetown, they had shared the chore, laughing and clowning around. The remembered sounds of their laughter echoed mockingly around her as she slowly rinsed the cups.

She retired when the dishes were put away. Scrupulously setting her alarm watch to awaken her in time for her shift at the wheel, she crawled into bed, seeking the oblivion of sleep. For a few hours, at least, she could escape.

Before going up to take her watch, she piled her books on her hastily made bunk. If Dominic was still using the vacant bunk when she was on watch, she didn't want him annoyed with her possessions covering it. She pulled on her sweater and turned off the light.

'You are always prompt, Miss Kent, I will say that,' he mocked her when she rose from the main cabin. Lexy ignored this and came to the helm. The breeze was up, snapping the sails, driving the Marybeth along at a fine clip. The sea was a bit heavier than she remembered at supper, and she was surprised she hadn't felt it in the forward bunk.

'You have to hold her hard on the course, tonight, Lexy, she wants to veer left.'

'Right.' She stepped in and took the wheel, bracing herself for the pull when Dominic released it. It was strong. She stood still, holding the wheel steady, the sloop on course. He watched her a moment, a pale wraith in the fitful light, then he softly taunted her, 'You missed your chance, Miss Kent, you should have acted faster, you know.'

She looked at him. What now?

'I'm a chivalrous man or like to think I am. You should have used my sleeping in the port bunk more to your advantage. Snuggled in with me one night. Compromised, I might have felt I owed you.'

Lexy's fingers tightened on the wheel, but she gave no further sign she had heard him.

'You should have tried before Joey came, however, because now the game's up.'

'I know, forewarned and forearmed,' she said tiredly. What was he trying to do? Why not go to bed and leave her alone.

'I don't think I'm such a great catch, but I can see why an old maid like yourself might try for anyone. You aren't getting younger, and must be getting tired of your, er, occupation.'

'Shut up!' she snapped.

He smiled, glad at last for some reaction from her, somehow his shaft had hit hard. 'You're here to work, just don't forget it. None of your wiles, they won't work.'

Lexy glanced at the soft light of the compass. They were right on the course he had plotted, but her wrists were beginning to ache with the strain of the wheel. She glanced again at Dominic. He seemed to be waiting for something; he was very still, poised as if to pounce. Bewildered she tried to guess what he wanted.

'Goodnight,' she said politely at last.

He hesitated another moment, turned, and without another word left the deck.

Lexy let out a sigh of relief and shifted her weight to counter the pull of the wheel more effectively. Reaching around, she grasped the wheel lock and snapped it on. The release of the pressure was heavenly on her wrists. She gazed out to sea, the phosphorescence of their wake glowing in the starlight. Whitecaps frothed here and there in the wind. The sloop was moving rapidly, the sails trimmed, the wind abeam. To the starboard, in the distance, other running lights were moving on a parallel course. Lexy wondered who was traveling on that boat and if the person on watch there felt as lonely as she did. Briefly she raised her hand and waved, smiling at her own foolishness. No one could see her in the dark. She checked the compass.

At half past four the wind died. It had been slowing for a while, but still moving the boat. She trimmed the sails again, coaxing as much from the breeze as she could. Then it died completely. Lexy checked their course, still on. She pulled in the mainsail, taut as it would go, no movement, no flutter, the boom swinging aimlessly now as the sea began to turn the boat to its whims. It was still running high and the swells were rocking the boat side to side now that it had lost its forward propulsion.

Damn, just what I need, she raged, lowering the jib, keeping the mainsail up, hoping for a breath of air. The boat was wallowing now, turned in the waves, at the mercy of their swells, of the current. She checked the compass again, they were turned off course now. She sat undecided for a moment, then checked the engine. The key was not in it. Dominic must have it with him. She'd have to wake him up and get it. Still she sat on the helm, delaying her move, reluctant to waken him, reluctant to face his scorn and dislike again.

Finally she forced herself up and into the cabin. Softly she went forward and reached for the door. It was locked. She stared at it in stupefaction for several minutes before the full significance of it hit her. Dominic had locked the door against her. She didn't know whether to laugh or scream in rage. She did neither. Taking a deep breath she rapped on the door.

'Dominic, open up,' she called, pounding on the door, 'Dominic!'

'Ummm, what d'you want?' a muffled voice came through.

'Open the door. I need the key,' she shouted back, pounding again. The door opened so abruptly she almost knocked on his chest.

'Oh. Sorry to wake you, Mr. Frazer,' she said politely gazing at a point just above his left shoulder, 'but we seem to have run out of wind and I thought. . .' she broke off as the boat dipped suddenly, corkscrewing in the trough, and she was thrown off balance, sitting down hard on the floor.

Dominic caught himself on the doorjamb. 'Whoa, we are wallowing. When did the wind die?' He came out of the forward cabin clad only in a pair of hastily drawn on jeans. He stepped neatly across Lexy and hastened topside. Quickly taking stock of the situation, he took the wheel, releasing the lock, yelling to Lexy to lower the mainsail. In only a couple of minutes the steady throb of the engine brought the sloop around and kept the bow straight on course. Lexy finished furling the sail and returned aft.

'If the wind freshens enough for you to feel it, run up the sail again and cut the engine, if not we'll run on gas power until we give out. If the seas weren't so heavy I'd leave us becalmed. There must be a storm somewhere.'

Lexy stepped in to the wheel, reaching for the lock. He knew anyway she had never held the heavy wheel before, what did she care if he saw her fasten it now. She wasn't out to impress him, not him nor anyone. When this job was finished, or she reached a fair-size town, she would leave, never seeing him again. In fact she would leave the whole West Indies, go to Canada or the United States.

Get far away from anyone who knew the name of Alexis Kent. She was not the green girl of eighteen this time. She had a little money and a lot more experience in the ways of the world and of men. She wouldn't make the same mistakes again—she knew better now. Next time she'd have a careful story prepared. Having no luck in people believing the true story, maybe she would have better luck with a complete fabrication.

'I'll try not to disturb your rest again, Mr. Frazer,' she bit out, bitter at the discovery of the locked door. Did he worry she would try to *compromise* him now?

He watched her in the faint light for a long minute, then turned and left the deck without a word.

She straightened her shoulders and stood tall, forcing her facial muscles into a serene, peaceful mask. No one would best her again, she vowed. She would do her work and pass on. Foolish dreams and vague regrets were for others, not Lexy Kent. She would take what the future held and turn it to her advantage—somehow.

5

She made no mention of the locked door at breakfast. A light breeze came up at dawn from the southwest and they were again using sail power by the time Dominic awoke. But only moving enough for steering, their actual progress was slow. They ate their meal in total silence, Dominic glaring at Lexy's serene countenance, not guessing the tremendous willpower she used to keep it so. As soon as she cleared the table, Dominic spread out his laptop and papers. He organized his notes, scattering stacks of papers here and there, and began to type.

Lexy grabbed a book and went topside. All morning the steady clicking of the keyboard drifted out on deck.

Dominic had his first chapter neatly mapped out and the words flowed from his mind to his fingertips. The noise didn't disturb Lexy, she soon ignored it, deep into a new mystery. Escaping her own thoughts and worries in the murder and maze of clues of the book.

The day was warm but not hot, moving as they were on the sea. While the breeze continued slight, the forward motion of the boat provided sufficient circulation to make it pleasant even in full sun. The swells were still large, but the white-capped waves had disappeared with the brisk wind. Again, the Marybeth was alone on the turquoise sea.

Lexy was dozing in the afternoon sun, her stomach growling when she heard Dominic's yell. She dared not intrude while he was working, even though she was hungry and thirsty. It was long past lunchtime and she wished she'd had the foresight to bring some food along to nibble on while she waited for him to get hungry enough to take a break.

'Lexy, lunch,' Dominic called.

She checked the wheel, scanned the sea, and went below. He was still typing, though more sporadically now, yellow foolscap scattered across the table. He glanced up, as her eyes grew accustomed to the dimmer interior light.

'I just want a sandwich or something. Put it on the table. You'll have to eat topside, I don't want to rearrange my papers.'

She turned and pulled out the bread, hurt afresh that he couldn't even bear to eat with her now. Silently she made his sandwich, took a beer from the cooler and set them in a small place cleared of papers near him. Her own sandwich she carefully carried topside with her soda. She couldn't eat it. She tried a bite, but the tears choked her, turning the bread to sawdust. She forced down the first bite, laying the sandwich back on the plate. She'd been hungry before, now she couldn't eat a bite.   Maybe later. She watched the waves of the sea; they sparkled and shimmered in the sunlight, dancing here and there as far as her eye could see.

Standing, she crossed to the rail, watching the wake, watching the smooth patch right behind the boat that veered out wider and wider as the boat continued along. If she fell over, would Dominic know she was gone? How long before he realized she wasn't on board? Idly she wondered if he would turn back and search for her. It wouldn't matter; if she went now, he'd never find her—the sea was such a vast, lonely place. He couldn't know where to search for her.

Escape. Escape of a sort.

A coward's way, she thought scornfully. Then, I'm so tired

and unhappy, I can't live like this. What's the point? It never gets better. Unconscious of time, she watched the water, memorized by the endless action of the sloop's wake, the swells as they rose and fell. The sea was her friend, warm and inviting. She'd spent long contented hours diving and swimming in it in the past. Wouldn't it stand her friend now? She leaned further out. It was so peaceful and quiet, except for the small smacking noise of the water against the hull. So peaceful.

'Drink your soda, Miss Kent, it's getting warm.' Dominic took her arm and turned her around, away from the stern, away from temptation, back to him and the boat, back to reality. He thrust her soda can into her hand.

Dumbly Lexy raised her eyes to his. Hers dulled and filled with pain and unhappiness; his with—was it worry?

No, even as she looked at him the blue hardened and became remote, withdrawn. She dropped her gaze, looking at the can now in her hand.

The beverage was warm—how long had she been standing at the rail? Well, that was out, for now at least. Things would get better. If she could only wait long enough. She took another sip, discovering she was still thirsty. Taking her time, careful not to look at the tall, silent, disapproving man beside her, she sipped her drink, finding it easy to swallow, finding it helped fill the void within her.

She went forward, sitting near the bow, resting against the wall of the cabin. Suddenly a picture of her grandfather flashed into her thoughts. Taking another sip of warm soda, she wondered how he was, if he ever gave any thought to her, to how she was faring, to where she was.

I don't even know if he's still alive, she thought with some surprise. He was well past seventy when she left. He could very well have passed on these last years and I wouldn't know. Maybe

I'll write to cousin Susan and find out.

But even as she thought it, she knew she wouldn't. He had sent her away, casting her from his family, severing all ties. It was not up to her to mend things. She could not, ever. She could only regret her actions and continue on. She flung her can overboard in a spurt of temper.

'Damn all men!' she gritted out.

Dinner was another quiet ordeal. Dominic yelled for Lexy to come and fix the food, then resumed his work. She glanced at him once or twice wondering what had brought him up on deck that afternoon. Surely he would be just as pleased to see the end of her? He didn't know she was there right now, so engrossed was he in his writing. What had interrupted him earlier?

His sporadic typing, ruffling of research notes and drumming of fingers while thinking got on Lexy's nerves as she quickly grilled some tomatoes, onions and pan- steaks. He ignored her totally, not looking at her, not talking to her. She put his plate carefully on some yellow paper near his elbow. Her head held high, she carried her own meal out on the deck, sitting by the wheel.

She was hungry. She attacked the mixed grill and enjoyed every bite. Missing lunch had only added to her hunger and she could have eaten seconds. She licked her lips when finished and sipped the iced fruit juice she had brought for herself. Watching a lone gull whirling in the air, she looked around for land. The sea remained smooth, no dark mass on the horizon anywhere. She shrugged bringing her eyes back to her juice.

Briefly she thought about her silent day. She had scarcely said a dozen words since Dominic had started the engine before daylight, and she made a wry grimace. If nothing else, when she finished this job she would have good references for joining that religious group which took vows of silence. She giggled a little at the thought, picturing her interview with the Mother Superior.

'Yes, I know I'd be right for the position, I have experience...' she said aloud to the imaginary figure. Dominic's typing paused. She looked nervously to the cabin, but the typing resumed. She stuck out her tongue and resumed her conversation.

'You see, Mother, I traveled for days on the ocean . . .' the typing stopped. She closed her mouth, a small giggle welling up inside. The typing resumed. '... with an odd author who thought. . .' Again the typing paused.

Lexy giggled, envisioning Dominic's head cocking to one side trying to ascertain if he were hearing voices. The typing began again. Lexy waited a minute, '. . . crew members should be . . .' She paused as he did, laughter breaking out. '. . . seen, but not heard . . When the typing stopped this time she lay back and gave in to her mirth.

A release from tension, making the situation seem far funnier than it actually was, caused Lexy to convulse with laughter. She rolled around on the seat, holding her sides, tears streaming. She found it hilariously funny.

Dominic's dark visage, with his raised eyebrow, appearing in the doorway, set her off again. She looked at him and laughed, looked away and brought herself under control; a quick look back, however, set her off again.

'What's funny?' he asked politely, standing in the doorway, his hair disordered as if he had run his fingers through it many times, his shirt opened to the waist.

Lexy looked at him, and laughed in his face. 'You are,' she gasped out, going into peals of laughter. She was limp with it, leaning back and letting go. Oh, it felt so good to laugh again.

She chuckled, eventually trailing off.

Dominic's face was carved from stone, granite-hard and unyielding. He watched her for a few moments, as gradually she subsided, a sidelong glance at him, though, renewed her chuckles.

He moved then, quickly, like the cat she had likened him to that first day. Reaching for her, his fingers bit into the soft flesh of her shoulders. He dragged her up and

Lexy's eyes widened briefly before his mouth began its assault on her. His lips were hard, pressing against hers forcing hers apart while his mouth ravaged hers. His fingers dug into her as he pulled her closer, releasing her shoulders to cradle her head; his other hand hard against the bare skin revealed by her swimsuit, drawing her up against the length of him. Lexy was very aware that only her bikini stood between her and Dominic. The hard muscles of his chest unyielding against her soft breasts, his stomach against her own. His lips continued their assault as he disregarded her feeble attempts to push away. Finally, he threw her contemptuously away from him. She stumbled back, and sat down hard on the bench. Raising her hand to her swollen lips, her dazed eyes sought his, seeking an explanation.

His breathing was ragged. He looked through her with smoldering eyes, raking her trembling figure, clad only in her brief bikini; and turned away as if in disgust. With her? With himself?

'Go to bed,' he ground out hoarsely, turning his eyes to the far horizon of the sea.

Lexy needed no further urging. She scampered off, slamming the door to the forward cabin and fumbling for the lock. Not permitting herself to think, she pulled on her nightshirt and slipped beneath the sheet. Only then did the scene replay itself over and over on her brain. His merciless kiss–for what?

For laughing? She sighed, rubbing her fingers lightly across her tender mouth. No, it was not for laughing.

Lexy took her turn at the wheel promptly at two without comment. Dominic looked hard at her, but she kept her head averted and pretended not to notice. She checked the compass, they had changed direction she noted, the sails were tightly trimmed, seeking the waning breeze, and at least the sea was calm now. If the wind died tonight she would toss out a sea anchor and let them sit until morning. She would not disturb him no matter what.

It was not necessary. The wind continued steady, if light, all night.

Lexy was surprised to see Dominic coming on deck at first light. She gave a startled gasp, he usually rose later. He looked at her. She was conscious of his strength and size against the small cabin door. His unruly hair fell across his face untidily, and unexpectedly she experienced a strong desire to brush it back, to run her fingers through its thickness. Aware of longings surging through her even as his blue eyes remained hard and watchful, Lexy remembered when they had been warm and friendly— before he had learned of her past. Her eyes dropped briefly to the tightly held lips of his mouth. She ran her tongue lightly over her still puffy lips, remembering the pain of his kiss. Once before, in Bridgetown, he had kissed her; and it had been sweet and promising. She disciplined her thoughts.

'Is something wrong?' She forced her voice to be polite.

'No.' He came out on deck, a dark blue turtleneck shirt encasing his torso, tight denim jeans on his muscular thighs. His sneakers made no noise as he crossed to the starboard rail and looked seaward. Lexy had not noticed the binoculars in his hand, but he raised them now and swept the horizon. Lowering them, he looked forward again, raising the glasses. A brief smile lit his face.

'The island I anchor near is almost dead ahead. We'll drop anchor before lunch,' he said, keeping his eyes on the faint speck on the horizon.

Lexy stared stonily ahead. What did it matter to her, any of it? She had to put in her time until they returned to Bridgetown, or another city large enough to enable her to get transportation away from the West Indies. She sat hunched up near the wheel, keeping watch on the sail and the steerage.

Dominic crossed over and sat beside her, as if some of his antagonism was gone, purged by the kiss he had inflicted last night. Nodding his head towards the horizon he spoke.

'It's a small coral island. There's a nice lagoon, sheltered and peaceful. We'll anchor in the lagoon, but can go ashore whenever we want. Robin used to go a lot— exploring, he said. I was working.'

'Is the island inhabited?' Lexy met the new truce halfway.

'No. Too far from the beaten track, and little fresh water on it.'

Lexy considered this. 'Is it just a rock then?'

'No, it's a regular island, has soil of a kind, sandy beach, lots of palm trees and all. Actually there is a large pond near the center of the island, but it's rain water that collects after storms as far as I can figure, not a spring originating on the island.' He slanted a look at her. 'It looks like everybody's dream of a tropical island.'

Everybody's dream. The words echoed in Lexy's brain later as Dominic maneuvered the boat through the channel entering the lagoon. It was a large horseshoe lagoon, unbelievably blue, with a wide outlet to the sea. Surrounding it, sandy white beaches extended back to the thick green plants, here and there a hibiscus splashed red or purple against the greens. To the left, a small hill rose in the distance, giving the island a sense of size.

'It's lovely. Beautiful,' she breathed, entranced with the setting. This was worth the years in the West Indies. It was pristine and untouched—a veritable paradise. She cocked her head at Dominic, complete with serpent, she thought, though his idea of the serpent present would be different from hers. No matter. She would fix his three meals a day, and endure his silence, to be able to enjoy and experience this lovely island. She looked eagerly to the water. This afternoon she would swim, maybe go ashore.

Oh, it would be fun. In spite of Mr. Dominic Frazer and his disapproval. She could hardly wait.

'Drop the sails, Lex,' Dominic barked as the sloop turned in the lagoon. She moved quickly, glad of his help a few minutes later. They worked well together, furling the canvas, snapping on the covers. It would be weeks before they would be used again. The anchor splashed down, the chain playing out until the blades caught in the ocean floor and held.

When everything was set topside, Lexy headed below, calling over her shoulder that she was fixing lunch. She rummaged around their supplies, fixing a quick meal, anxious to be through and in the water. She noticed the pink bakery box, pushed back in the cooler. A moment of regret gave her pause. How happy she had been when she had bought the cakes for their desserts. How long ago it seemed, though in fact it had only been a couple of days. Maybe they could have them for dessert tonight.

She put Dominic's lunch on the table, carrying hers on deck. He was standing casually at the rail, looking to shore. She saw he had pulled off his shirt, his brown shoulders and chest exposed to the sun. It was noticeably warmer now that they had stopped, but not unpleasantly so. He turned when he heard her and cocked his eyebrow.

'No lunch for the boss?'

'I left it on the table, where you usually have it.'

'Well, I'm not having it there today. Go and get it,' he ordered pleasantly.

Lexy hesitated, she wasn't his servant, he could get his own plate. Her lips were opened to tell him so when she caught his brooding stare at her mouth, and she remembered her experience of last night. She didn't want a repeat. If he ever kissed her again she wanted it to be with affection, not anger, or scorn or whatever he was feeling last night.

'All right,' she muttered putting down her food and returning for his.

They ate in silence, but Lexy didn't care. She was studying the island from the boat, excited with the thought of swimming the short distance to it this afternoon. She knew Robin had been all over it, but she could pretend she was its discoverer, the first to touch its white sands, to see its mysterious interior.

'Miss Kent.' Dominic's stern voice interrupted her fantasy. She brought herself back and looked at him. 'Two rules here, you don't swim alone and you tell me where you are heading if you go to the island.'

She frowned. 'I assure you, Mr. Frazer, I can handle myself in the water.'

'Even the most expert swimmer can run into trouble. If I don't have your word,' here he stopped and gave her a derisive look, 'your promise, such as it is, that you'll follow the rules, I'll lock you in the cabin when I'm working.'

She felt the familiar rage welling up in her, the hatred for the position she was in. She started to speak out, but he was right, darn him, swimmers should be in pairs, it was a common sense safety rule.

'All right,' she conceded with poor grace. 'Can we swim today?'

'Sure, soon as lunch settles. There's a dinghy ashore, we'll swim in and check it out, bring it to the ship if it's still seaworthy. You can swim back while I row. In fact you can swim any time you want as long as you let me know. If I'm not ready to swim, I'll keep an eye out for you from the boat.'

She smiled shyly at this, only to be frozen by his cold look. Changing the subject, she asked about the dinghy.

'We brought it from my aunt's. Her place is about a day's sail from here. It's handy if you want to go for a walk, so that you can reach the beach without getting wet. We usually leave it here between visits; it keeps and saves the bother of hauling it behind us all the time. Do you row?'

'Yes.' She was still smarting under his snub. She would remember her place from now on and not give him any cause to suspect her of 'using her wiles' on him. She left him and went to change into her bikini.

She was at the rail, ready to dive in, when he spoke to her next. 'Anxious to swim, Miss Kent?'

She said, in exasperation, 'Sometimes you call me Lexy, other times Miss Kent, can't you be consistent? What's wrong with Lexy? Can't we ever be friends again?'

He looked at her for a long minute. 'I doubt we'll ever be friends, Lexy, but we very well may be lovers before the book is written. So Lexy it is,' he smiled sardonically, watching the faint color rise in her face.

Shaking her head, she refuted his assertion that they might become lovers. Against her will she imagined how it would be to lie next to his long length, feel his hands on her, his mouth teaching her, touching her, giving her pleasure. She shivered against the picture, turning away whispering frantically, 'No, no!'

denying the image even to herself. Not for anything would she let him know how much she would have liked it, had circumstances been different.

'Can we swim now?' she asked, her back to him. Starting, she felt his fingers trace down her spine, resting on her lower back, just at her bikini line. She wanted to move away from his disturbing touch, but her legs wouldn't obey her brain. She trembled. If he didn't move, didn't stop–

'You go in, I'll give you a head start and race you to shore,' he said lazily.

Diving, she took off like the devil himself was after her. Lexy was a strong, accomplished swimmer, her work with Miles Jackson had seen to that. She swam hard, straight for the closest stretch of beach, straining to reach the land, conscious only of her overwhelming desire to put as much distance between herself and Dominic as she could. She could hear him coming, but wasted no time trying to locate him in the water, all her energies focused on reaching the shore, reaching it first, as if she had to in order to prove something.

Her feet touched land. She scrambled up on shore, turning to land on the warm sand, Dominic was still in the water.

'I won,' she cried gleefully. 'Ha, ha, Dominic, I won!'

He reached the white beach, not pounded by the surf, but only caressed by the gentle water lapping the sand much like a small lake. He strode out of the water, rivulets streaming from his hair and shoulders, looking Lexy over from head to toe.

'Very pretty, my dear,' he jeered, 'but the lovely heroine sprawled so enticingly on the beach awaiting the virile hero is just a little too contrived, don't you think? I will choose the time and place to make love to you,' he stated arrogantly, ignoring her gasp of outrage. How dare he think such a thing about her!

'Come on, let's check the dinghy,' he turned and walked down the beach.

'I won't need the convent,' she muttered darkly as she rose to her feet and followed him down the beach, glaring at his frame. 'I'll murder him first and jail will be my destination. How dare he think I was enticing him. Blast his ego!'

Far above the high-tide line, nestled into the brush, they found the dinghy, overturned to keep the water from settling in. Dominic turned it over on its keel.

'Grab the bow and push,' he said taking a firm grip on the flat aft section, nearer the sea, and pulling. Lexy complied and slowly the little wooden dinghy moved to the sea. Afloat it took on a little water, but Dominic dismissed the idea of a leak.

'It'll be fine once the planks swell again. I'll hold it here, go check the bushes for the oars.'

Finding them with no problem, Lexy dragged them to the water's edge.

'Here,' she shot them out to him, one at a time. 'I'm going to swim some more.'

'Okay. I dropped the ladder over the stern before I came. Come aboard when you're tired.' He stepped into the dinghy and started rowing easily back to the Marybeth.

Lexy dived into the clear, blue waters aware of the soft feel of it against her warm skin. The top six inches or so were very warm, and when she floated it was like a bath. Jack-knifing down, she could feel the water grow cooler as she went deeper— it was so refreshing and pleasant. She opened her eyes to the coral bottom and exotic tropical fish. The salt water stung a little, but it was a wonderland, worth the irritation. Tomorrow she would bring the face mask to see more clearly.

Generally the lagoon averaged only twenty feet in depth, falling off here and there into deeper troughs. Lexy swam until she was tired, then floated on the surface, reluctant to leave the watery playground. Lazily she circled the boat, finding the ladder extended on the flat stern board. Slowly she climbed it.

Dominic was typing when she pulled herself on deck. She padded forward and lay on the cabin roof, drying in the late afternoon sun. Lying on the warm roof she wondered again what his book was about this time, wondered where she would be when she read it. Would it always bring back memories of these days on the Marybeth? Or would she one day, in the far future, forget?

Dominic ate dinner at his typewriter while Lexy ate topside. Back to square one, she thought as she watched the island. Maybe tomorrow she would go exploring, do it in the morning when it was cooler, swim in the afternoon.

She had one of the cakes for dessert, a luscious cream-filled éclair. Dominic had declined, shuffling through his papers, checking on a fact. Lexy watched him thoughtfully. Perhaps he wasn't ignoring her so much as a punishment for her past sins, but was just fully engrossed in his creative work. Maybe.

'I'm going to bed,' she announced, standing by the table. 'Do you need anything from the forward cabin?'

He looked up, glanced out of the window. It was still light outside.

'So early?'

'I'm going to read first. Do you need bedding or something?'

'Yes, get me some from the port bin. My pillow too. Just put the stuff on the sofa. I'll make up the bed when I'm ready,' he turned back to his laptop.

Lexy awoke in the night, tearing pains in her abdomen. She was bathed in sweat, sharp pains stabbing again and again. She groaned, drawing her knees up, trying to ease the racking agony. Oh, the pain came again and again almost in a wave. Suddenly she felt sick. She would have to run to the head, please let her be in time. Staggering from her bunk she grabbed for the door. Ohhh, doubled over against the agony in her stomach, she reached the small bathroom alongside the galley—reached it just in time.

She was sick again and again. Vomiting up her supper, heaving long after her stomach was empty, trying to escape the stabbing in her stomach. She was wet with sweat.

'Oh, God,' she thought, 'am I dying?' It was so awful, so painful. Finally the vomiting eased. Lexy took a deep breath. Another. She was still crouched on the floor of the head, her hands pressing hard against her stomach, trying vainly to ease the pain. Oh, she couldn't stand it any longer. She moaned softly against another wave. How would she get back to bed?

'Lexy?' Dominic's voice came from the dark. In another minute the cabin lights were flicked on and he was bending over her, lifting her and carrying her to the double bed the sofa had made.

'Lexy, what's wrong?' He laid her down gently.

'Oh, the pain, I'm in such pain,' she gritted out, her teeth clenched, her knees drawn up against her chest, her hands holding her stomach convulsively. 'Oh, Dominic, please help me, please.'

'Where, Lexy? Where do you hurt?' His eyes concerned, searching for a wound or injury.

'My stomach,' she groaned, rocking herself back and forth on the bed. Would nothing ease the cramps? She was so hot, so hot! What was wrong with her?

Dominic got a damp rag from the bathroom and wiped her face gently, wiped her neck. He slipped into the bed, turning her away from him and pulling her curved back against his chest, his hands encircling her, splaying out against her stomach, kneading it softly, trying to ease her suffering.

'It's not appendicitis, is it?' he asked in her ear, cradling her in his arms, his warm hands helping a little to ease the pain.

Shaking her head she answered gasping, 'No . . . had them out when I was sixteen . . . oh, please help me, please, I hurt so much!' She doubled over as a fresh wave hit her, sweat breaking out again.

'Must be something you ate.'

'I don't know.' She was panting now. 'You ate what I did.' She lay very still for a few minutes, the pain just tolerable. She lay immobile, afraid to move, to breath, lest it bring on the pain again.

Dominic's hands were caressing, pushing gently against her abdomen, kneading the softness of her belly, feeling her relax.

'Is this a clever way of getting into my bed?' he asked, his mouth inches away from her ear, his tone whimsical.

'I knew . . . you wouldn't be able to . . . resist me like this,' she retorted, taking shallow breaths, her eyes wide, awaiting the returning pain. She only felt discomfort now, an aching relief from the sharp shafts of a few minutes ago. Slowly she tried breathing again.

Even as he chuckled at her sally, the sharp pain came again. She cried out, tensing herself against its onslaught. Unable to stifle the moan in her throat.

'Did you eat one of those blasted cream cakes—' he asked suddenly, feeling her nod in reply. 'Well, of all the foolish things. It's probably gone bad by now. The cooler doesn't keep things as cold as a refrigerator. The box was left out most of the day we sailed, too. We, er, had other things to think of.'

'I have . . . such a weakness for ... cream cake,' she gasped out against the suffering. 'Oh, Dominic, can't you do something. . . anything... it hurts so much.' She was panting again, trying to hold off from the harsh reality, all her mind focused on the stabbing torment within her.

'I don't have anything for food poisoning, Lexy. It'll pass, in only a little while, it'll pass.' His strong arms molded her to him, his hands trying to ease her hurt.

'How long?' she panted.

'A couple of hours, I don't know.'

'I can't stand it. Dominic, don't you have something I could take, something that might help? '

'I'll fix you some tea.' He carefully disentangled himself and eased off the bunk.

'No, I feel sick again, I couldn't drink it.'

He disappeared into the head for a minute, returning with a small pill in his hand. He got a small glass of water from the galley and came back to the bed.

'Try the pill, put it in your mouth and I'll help you sip the water. Just a little. Try to keep it down. It'll help.'

She took the pill, tried to raise up for the water, but needed Dominic's arm under her shoulders to hold her up enough so that the water didn't spill. She took the glass and tried a small sip, then a tremulous smile came to her drawn face, and her tormented eyes met his.

'Not the fancy courtesan tonight,' she whispered, trying for humor.

'No,' he smiled gently, 'but don't lose heart, my darling tramp, there's always tomorrow.' Dominic flicked out the light and climbed back into the bed, holding her again, his hands rubbing her gently, comfortingly. She tensed again.

'It's not working,' she whispered.

'Shhh, it's a sleeping pill. If it will knock you out, the pain will be gone by morning. Try to relax.'

She felt the pain again, but not as sharp, her head swimming a little. Incredibly, the pill worked. In only a little while Lexy was asleep, curled in a ball, held safe and firm in the curve of Dominic's arm.

6

The sun danced across her eyes, was gone, came again, was gone. Frowning, she moved her head from its reach, and slowly opened her eyes. The rapid clicking of the keyboard penetrated her consciousness and she awoke fully. Looking around, she saw she was still lying on Dominic's bed, the sheet a tangled mess. The gentle rocking of the Marybeth caused the sun to shift its light from the porthole, now on her cheek, now near her head.

Cautiously she straightened her legs, there was no pain. There was a small ache in her stomach, but the awful agonizing pain was gone. She rolled over, raising her head slightly. She could just see the top of Dominic's head bent over his laptop. The steady clicking evidence that he was in full spate and in a world of his own.

Slowly she sat up. Not too bad, a little weak, but that was to be expected. She stood up, the movement catching Dominic's eye.

'How do you feel?' he asked.

'All right.'

'Good.' He watched her for a moment, then nodded and resumed typing, oblivious again to-her presence.

Lexy made her way forward, and dressed in the day before's shirt and jeans. She sat for a moment on the bunk, gathering strength. She'd feel better after breakfast, but at that thought her stomach turned over. She wrinkled her nose. Food sounded awful. Shakily, she made her way to the galley; Dominic would want to eat, maybe she would feel better soon.

He looked up, seeing the pale face, over-large eyes, and shaky stance of the slight figure. She looked drawn and haggard.

'Just fix tea and crackers,' he said. 'That's all you'll be able to keep down right now.'

'But your breakfast.'

'I ate a while ago.'

She nodded, glad for the reprieve.

'Thank you for . . . for your help last night,' she said watching the teakettle heat.

'No problem. I tossed out the remaining cakes,' he added, a smile threatening.

Lexy gave a wan smile at this, but said nothing. She took her meager breakfast topside, sitting on the cabin roof and looking towards the island. As she drank the strong tea and nibbled on the crackers, she wondered if she would have the strength that afternoon to row to the island. Dominic said there was a fresh-water pond inland. If she could get to it, she could wash her clothes. She only had two sleep shirts and had put the second one on clean last night. She had several other things to wash out, too.

She would try later, but right now it was heavenly just to sit in the sun, its warmth soothing, the air soporific, only the steady drone of the keyboard disturbing the silence. Lexy lay back, and drifted off to sleep.

She felt better after lunch, sticking to the diet Dominic had recommended, but eating it more confidently.

Now was the time to try the island, she decided. Dominic was engrossed with his work, and she didn't want to interrupt, but conscious of her promise, knew she had to. She gathered her clothes and some soap, bundling them together.

'Dominic?'

'Ummm?' He did not look up.

'I'm going ashore, where is the pond?'

'Ummm?' He finished typing his line.

'Dominic!'

'What?' He focused on her, as if coming from a distance.

'I want to find the pond on the island, which direction?'

'Left, towards the hill, at the bottom of it. There's a path.' He turned back to his book, forgetting her.

She rolled her eyes and, stopping to gather up his sheets, went out. Lexy had no trouble getting the dinghy ashore, nor in finding the pond. There was a well-defined trail; obviously Robin had traveled often to the fresh water.

After washing her clothes and the sheets in the clear cold water, she wondered if they would dry better spread on the bushes around the pond, or on the railings of the boat. She opted for the boat, having nothing to do on the island while they dried. On the ship she could get a book, take another nap or maybe swim, though the latter didn't hold as much appeal as it had yesterday. She was still a little shaky, and it would be a while before she would splurge on cream cakes again.

She gathered everything and made her way carefully down the path, enjoying the sights of the soaring palms, the fragrance of the frangipani, the color of the flowers blooming in profusion along the side of the path. She wondered if the seeds of these plants came on the wind, or if someone long ago had planted them to provide color in a perfect land.

She reached the beach, her arms tired from the weight of the wet clothes and sheets, obviously she was not yet fully restored from her food poisoning. She watched the sand, looking for shells, perfect ones that others had overlooked. She smiled at her foolishness, what would she do with a shell if she found one? She'd had dozens, and all unusual specimens, when working with Miles, but she had left them all behind.

Balancing the wash on her lap, she rowed to the ship.

She giggled a little in anticipation at the expression on Dominic's face when he saw the laundry fluttering from the lines of the Marybeth. Two lacy bras, and several lacy panties in addition to her sleep shirts were waving in the afternoon breeze. Dominic's sheets she draped over the railing, trying to keep them from brushing on the deck. They were dripping wet, but Lexy hoped they would be dry by night.

She went below to change into her bikini, even with her nap that morning; she felt nothing would be better than to lie in the sun. She told Dominic she was back when passing through but didn't think the fact registered with him.

Taking a book in case she decided to read, she crossed the deck, lying on the flat cabin roof. The words danced before her eyes. Giving up quickly, she turned to lay on her stomach, drifting to sleep, her arms pillowing her head.

A soft tug at her back brought her drowsily awake. Dominic was standing on the deck, leaning over her. He traced a finger lightly across her back, from side to side.

'You should unfasten your top so you don't get this light line,' he said, drawing his finger across it again, the fastening released.

'Go away,' she muttered. Darn him, why not leave her alone. 'Go write your story.'

'Umm, I need a break.' He drew his finger across her back again. Lexy stiffened.

'Stop it,' she continued, remaining on her stomach for modesty's sake.

'Make me,' he said, doing it again deliberately.

Lexy sat up quickly, her back towards him, her arms across her chest, holding her brief top in place. 'Go away, Dominic, don't tease,' she said, her voice catching in her throat.

Slowly, he sat beside her on the roof, reaching around to turn her slightly towards him. He was only wearing a pair of cut-offs, his skin warm on Lexy's shoulder where he touched her. She must still be feeling the effects of the food poisoning, because her stomach was churning, she was growing weak all over. She glanced at Dominic; his eyes were fixed on her lips, her mouth. She could scarcely breath.

'Please . . .' she whispered as he drew her nearer, his head blotting out the sun, his mouth claiming hers. Slowly drawing her into his arms, into his embrace, his kiss was a sweet caress.

Lexy felt on fire. His mouth evoked pleasures beyond her dreams as he kissed her long and deep. She returned his pressure, her mouth moving beneath his, her arms dropping their guarding position to reach out and draw him closer. He pulled her across his legs, kissing her languorously, passion rising between them. Generously Lexy gave herself to him, reveling in his touch, delighting in his hold, his hands warm and firm against her ribs.

She loved him! The knowledge exploded in Lexy like a bomb. How it had happened, she didn't know, but it would be all right now. Oh, she loved him so. Eagerly she kissed him back, trying to convey her feelings to him, longing for verbal confirmation he felt the same. He had to. This kiss was nothing like the one before.

Slowly he drew back, still holding her, withdrawing to gaze into her eyes, luminous and soft, looking up at him with her heart in her eyes.

His mouth twisted as he looked at her. 'Which of your men taught you to kiss like that, sweetheart? So well and with such abandonment.'

Had Lexy been slapped hard across the face she could not have been more shocked—or hurt. Her eyes darkened in disbelief and pain. Surely he didn't think— But of course he did.

'Full marks to you, darling, you're good,' he said bitterly.

'No! Damn you!' She wrenched herself from his arms, scrambling to fasten her top. She felt crushed. She had thought her love must shine through; she had given her all to him, and he thought she was playing him. Tears of humiliation coursed down her cheeks. How he would laugh if he learned of her love, how he would mock.

Before she could think of anything to say, she heard a low throbbing break into the tense atmosphere. She cocked her head, searching for the location of the sound. Was it a plane? A helicopter? No, it was closer. She turned, isolating the noise. Slowly, around the point, a large cruiser came into view, its gleaming white sides a beautiful contrast to the deep blue of the lagoon. Slowly, inexorably, she nosed her way in. The lagoon was large, capable of holding dozens of such craft, yet it felt a direct invasion of privacy when the boat was fully in. Lexy watched as the motors slowed, and the cruiser swung around.

'Damn!' Dominic rose and came to stand by Lexy, his eyes narrowed as he assessed their neighbor. The boat was a sixty-foot Chriscraft luxury yacht, ocean going, and from the signs of antennae and radar, fully equipped. The pilot drove it towards them, stopping sufficiently far away so as not to interfere with their anchor line. The engines cut and the prevailing silence descended again.

The skipper appeared on deck, cupping his hands and yelling across the space.

'Ahoy, mind if we anchor here for a night or two?'

'It'll be all right for one or two,' Dominic called back. He watched them drop anchor, and then turned, noticing for the first time Lexy's laundry hanging from the lines and rigging of the sloop.

'Good God, what's that?' A sardonic grin crossed his face. He looked from the fragile lacy scraps to Lexy, who was standing near by. He raked her figure, as if stripping her bikini from her and visualizing her in the flimsy pieces. She tried to out stare him, but dropped her gaze first. Damn him, she thought, aching to be in his arms again.

'I told you I was doing the laundry,' she said quietly.

He laughed, glancing at the rigging again, then at the cruiser. 'What will the neighbors think?' He sketched a smile at her and disappeared below as calm and composed as if nothing had happened.

With Dominic resuming his typing, Lexy wandered aft and sat at the helm, watching the new boat. She could spot figures moving about, but wasn't able to see very clearly. She lay back again and dozed in the warmth, trying to forget Dominic's kiss, his hurtful words. Her tongue ran lightly across her lips, and she sighed. The kiss was hard to ignore. She wished he felt for her a small bit of what she felt for him. She never expected to fall in love again. This time she should know better. But the heart had its own way about things. How much heartache would she bear when they parted?

Lexy was surprised when she went to dinner to find Dominic had cleared a portion of the table and expected her to eat with him. Lest she should have any ideas, he quickly informed her, it was so he could supervise her eating.

'Next time you come to my bed,' he continued, 'I don't want you so sick.'

She kept her back to him, her head high as she finished serving the plates and ignored his insulting comment. She would not let him get a rise out of her with his taunting threats. She would totally ignore him for a change.

Placing the dishes precisely on the table, she sat reluctantly opposite him. She wouldn't deign to reply to his suggestions— soon he would tire and leave her alone. She'd made another mistake today, assuming he cared for her as she did for him. Assuming his kisses meant something more than male lust. She vowed to watch that in the future. Silly daydreams were just that. Not to be taken seriously.

'How's your book coming?' she asked politely, seeing the growing pile of printed papers.

'It's coming.'

There was silence as they ate.

'I wonder where they're from,' Lexy murmured gazing out of the porthole at the other boat. The Marybeth had swung around with the tide and the newcomers could be seen from the port windows.

'I don't know, but don't go getting any ideas about changing ships. You're signed on with me for the duration,' he bit out.

She looked at him in surprise.

'The owner of that ship has a tidy bit of cash, obviously. As this berth didn't work out exactly as you planned, it's only natural you'd be looking out for your future, but it's not on, this time, sweetheart.'

'Shut up,' she snapped back. 'I wasn't thinking any such thing. Your mind is as foul as your cousin's. I offered to tell you the truth, but no, you would rather believe a pack of lies told about something Joey knew very little about. Stop baiting me.' She threw her napkin on the table and walked with what dignity she had left to the forward cabin.

Ten minutes passed in which Lexy lay back and wondered how she could finish her dinner with Dominic sitting opposite her. She smiled a little sadly, she wouldn't have this worry tomorrow, he'd clutter up the table again and expect her to eat on deck.

The knock on the door startled her. 'It's all yours, I'm going ashore.'

She opened the door a few minutes later to find the main cabin deserted. She finished her cold dinner and fixed herself a cup of tea. Cleaning the galley while the water boiled, she shut her mind to the thoughts churning through. Taking her tea topside she looked to the beach. The dinghy was drawn up on the sand, near it was another.

She sat on the cabin roof, sipping her tea, trying to see where Dominic and whoever had used the second dinghy were. Obviously inland somewhere, neither was visible from the boat. She was there quite some time before they appeared, from the direction of the pond. There were two men walking with Dominic, their features indiscernible at this distance, and one man had a decided paunch. They continued talking for several more minutes before Dominic shook hands and left them on the beach.

When he reached the sloop he joined Lexy on the roof, his eyes cool and aloof again. Let him begin it, she thought, masking her feelings and presenting a collected appearance, yet inwardly she was trembling. Just let him start it and she would throw the rest of her tea at him.

'We've been invited over for drinks after dinner tomorrow,' he said.

'Oh?'

'Umm. They wanted to know if I owned the island. I told them no, but a friend of mine did, but I didn't think he would mind if they stayed a day or two. They seem nice enough, but time will tell.'

'What does that mean?' she asked, ever conscious of a possible insult.

'A lot of pleasure crafts carry people who have loud parties far into the night. I'm here for peace and quiet. We'll see how it goes. As long as they don't bother me, I don't care if they stay.'

'And if you don't like them, you tell them to leave?' she asked.

'That's right.'

'Why didn't you tell me to leave?' she persisted.

'Oh, come on, Lexy, you know why. I needed a crew. I had made my plans and didn't see why I had to change them because of some cheap little tramp,' he ground out harshly.

Slowly, she arose and went to bed.

Lexy avoided Dominic as much as she was able the next day as she swam and sunbathed. It went against her grain to get his permission to swim, but she knew the alternative and had no doubt he would carry out his threat. He was typing, she could hear it from the water, but every fifteen minutes or so he was on the deck, checking that she was all right.

She had taken the snorkel, face mask and fins from one of the topside lockers after breakfast and had begun her explorations. It was exhilarating to be diving again and she wished they had some scuba gear, she was impatient with the times she had to surface for air. Sea anemones, urchins and coral shapes littered the floor of the lagoon. Bright, colorful, shy fish darted here and there before her as she challenged them in their native habitat. She found a couple of conch shells, perfect and large, their pale pink inner shells a soft glow against the white. She put them in the dinghy to save climbing on board the sloop.

'Lexy!' She turned from surfacing to see Dominic beckoning her to the boat. Reluctant to pause, she swam over.

'What?'

'Lunch.'

'What time is it?' Surely not noon already.

'After one, and I'm hungry. Aren't you? You've been diving for hours.'

She considered as she pulled off the face mask and reached down to unhook the fins.

'I guess I am. I had no idea it was so late. It's such fun, you see.'

'Come up now, though.'

He stood near the ladder, watching her as she left the water, her skin wet and shiny, her brief bikini plastered to her slight figure. Lexy swallowed, conscious of his eyes on her, remembering yesterday when his hands had been on her, evoking sweet sensations. She met his gaze bravely, then let her eyes wander insolently over him. He was wearing his cut-offs again, riding low on his hips, faded and short. She met his eyes again, surprised to find them brimming with amusement, and she looked away confused.

'Go fix lunch, and bring it up here, it's hot below.'

'Okay.' She was glad to escape.,

While they were eating, Lexy asked how he knew when to check on her all the time. 'You do get so absorbed in your writing sometimes.'

'Simple, I made a go-check-Lexy sign and put it in as a header. I check, then type that page.'

She smiled at this; delighted that he took her safety so seriously. Daringly she asked, 'Can I read what you've written so far?'

'No.'

'But I like your stuff, Dominic, I've read all your books.'

'I know, I've seen the beat-up copies in your library.'

She smiled shyly. 'I've read most of them more than once.'

'I'm glad you like them.'

'I'm sure I'll like this one, too. Please let me see.'

'No, I don't let people see the books before they're published. They say how good they are, but don't you think a little more of this or a little more of that would work? Then what if someone doesn't like something? I don't want to be influenced or put off by some amateur's point of view. No, Lexy, I don't let people have previews.'

She was quiet, wondering if he were speaking from experience, or if he were just visualizing what might happen. She looked out to the island, unable to imagine Dominic being influenced by someone else, especially not with his own thoughts and words. He was too strong, too confident in his own self.

'I'm at a stopping place now; I'm going to the island this afternoon. Why don't you rest after your morning's exertions?' Dominic said casually as he drained his beer and set the bottle on the tray she had brought up. 'We might be up late tonight.'

'Right, maybe I'll read a little.' She was disappointed he hadn't asked her to accompany him. They weren't at loggerheads at this moment and she'd relish some time in his company when they weren't fighting.

As she rinsed the lunch dishes, she heard him leave. She saw him reach the beach, pull up the dinghy and wander off into the interior. An idea hit her and, drying her hands, she turned slowly and approached the table. Almost reverently she reached for the stack of printed pages lying face down on the table. A quick glance over her shoulder and she took them into her cabin, closing and locking the door.

An hour and a half later she stole out and replaced the pages as nearly like she found them as she could. Then returned to her bunk. The story was good, as captivating and enthralling as any of his others. She marveled that he could put words together so well, make ordinary letters paint such vivid pictures on her mind.

The setting was the jungles of South America, the objective an abandoned mine. She wondered if he had actually gone there for his background research, actually cut a trail in the rain forest. She wished she could ask him, but he would be furious if he found she had read his manuscript, especially right after he had expressly forbidden it. She smiled dreamily, it was a wonderful story thus far, she couldn't wait to read more to see how it progressed, to see how it ended.

After dinner Dominic rowed them across the lagoon to the cabin cruiser. He wore a shirt the exact shade of blue as his eyes, bringing them into startling prominence in his dark face. Lexy wore one of her new tops, bright red, and skin-tight white jeans. Her hair was bleached almost blonde from the days in the sun and her skin had a deep tan. She felt quite festive and was looking forward to a pleasant visit.

'Watch how you walk and sit in those jeans,' Dominic admonished helping her into the dinghy. 'They look as if a good deep breath will rip them stem to stern.'

'They are not that tight,' she automatically defended. 'Just snug.'

'Ha! Just don't go flaunting them before our host,' he warned, setting in the oars and beginning to row.

'You met them yesterday,' she said, ignoring his last comment as unworthy of reply. 'What are they like? Where are they from?'

'The yacht's owner, Robert Driscoll, hails from Miami Beach, Florida, where he is a successful hotelier in a thriving tourist area. The oh-so-eligible Bob Driscoll is a bachelor and swimming in lard, from what they said. His guests are Samuel and Judy Martin. Judy is Bob's sister. Sam's in some sort of public relations work. They seemed like nice enough people.'

'What were they doing on shore yesterday?'

'Just wandering around. I showed them some of the highlights, and we talked. Judy wasn't on the jaunt, I've yet to meet her.'

'Ahoy, good taxi service you have.' A jovial voice greeted them from the stern of the cruiser. Lexy looked up and waved, a pleasant smile on her face. In no time she and Dominic were aboard and he was introducing her to their host.

'Bob, this is Lexy Kent, best crewman in the Indies. Lexy, Bob Driscoll of Miami Beach.'

She was astonished at Dominic's unexpected praise.

'Hello, Mr. Driscoll, nice to meet you.' Lexy extended her hand to their host. He was not as tall as Dominic, yet not precisely a small man. His ruddy complexion was topped by a thatch of reddish hair; his blue eyes, milder than Dominic's, beamed good naturedly; his handshake was firm and enthusiastic.

'Glad to meet you, little lady, glad to meet you. Call me Bob. Dominic and I are on first names. Come on, come on, take a seat. Judy! Sam!' He raised his voice calling the others. Waving a hand to several chairs surrounding a low table he turned to a rolling bar sitting in front of the control panel, obviously put away somewhere when the cruiser was moving.

Lexy looked around her with interest. The aft deck of the cruiser was spacious, over twelve feet wide and almost twice as long. She knew cruisers allocated space differently from sailboats, but all the same, this amount of room was almost indecent on a boat.

'What'll you folks have?' Bob turned from the bar.

'Scotch over, please,' Dominic said assisting Lexy to a chair, pulling his in close to her.

'Coke, please, Bob,' Lexy said. 'I'm just getting over food poisoning and don't want any more trouble.'

'That can be nasty, you all right?' He turned, concern wrinkling his face.

'Fine, now.'

'Good, aren't you the one I saw swimming today, mostly underwater, it looked like.'

She smiled. 'Yes. I love to swim.'

'You're good, too.'

'Lexy used to be the right-hand man for one of our eminent marine biologists here in the West Indies,' Dominic interjected smoothly. 'She worked for him for several years, and gained a lot of experience, swimming as well as some more domestic traits, eh, Lexy?'

Lexy flushed at the veiled insult, but Bob Driscoll didn't appear to find anything amiss.

'Well, fancy that. I say you must be a good crewman all round, sounds like quite a fascinating occupation.' Bob stopped mixing the drinks while he looked at Lexy, admiration on his face.

'Hello.' 'Hi.' Sam and Judy Martin joined them on the deck. Sam was the one with the paunch Lexy had seen last evening. He looked a few years older than Bob, whom Lexy placed at about forty-five, Sam's hair was thinning, and his face was pale compared with everyone else's tanned skins. Judy Martin was in her late thirties. Her relationship to her brother proclaimed in her red hair, worn short and curly. She was friendly and warm in her welcome when Bob made the introductions.

'Dominic Frazer and Lexy, er . . .' He fumbled for her name.

'Kent,' Dominic said, standing when Judy appeared.

'Right, my sister and brother-in-law, Judy and Sam Martin. Judy and Sam, Dominic and Lexy. We're all friends now. Sit down, sit down.' He distributed drinks, put peanuts and chips on the low round table and sat down himself.

'You've been here in this lagoon before, I understand, Dominic,' Judy was interested to know.

'Yes, several months out of each year,' he smiled. She was sitting on his right side, showing off her tanned legs in a very brief pair of shorts.

'And you, Lexy, do you come as often?'

'No, this is my first time here. I'm crewing for Dominic.'

'Can't handle the boat with only one man, eh?' Bob asked.

'Not really. In good weather, maybe, but it's best to carry a backup. Lexy's a good sailor, if nothing else, and knows enough to handle the sloop by herself if she had to.'

Lexy glared at him, why didn't he stop with the hints, the vague insults. Sooner or later one of the others would find something odd in his way of responding.

This information brought forth a spate of questions from Bob and Sam as to what Lexy had done, where she and Miles had searched for marine data, and how she had adjusted to life on a boat most of the time—usually women had so many knick-knacks, or so Sam said with a fond glance at his wife, that they didn't know how she could do it.

Lexy was glad to turn the conversation to safer channels and happily related some of her experiences working with Miles, the discoveries they had made, the long, painstaking observation and documentation needed to produce a strong report, acceptable to all as an accurate representation of what they were researching.

'Her experiences are varied, more so than she is relating now,' Dominic put in silkily as she paused.

Lexy ignored him.

'So it is not so unusual for a gal to crew a sail-boat hereabouts, then?' Bob finished.

'Except perhaps with such an attractive, single man,' Judy threw in teasingly.

'I shall have to look to my reputation,' Lexy smiled gaily at their banter.

'Honey-child, you don't have a reputation,' Dominic put in evenly, his eyes glittering as they met hers. 'You lost yours years ago.'

Lexy flushed scarlet with humiliation. She dropped her eyes, unable to force a sound beyond her tight throat; her chest so constricted she could scarcely draw a breath. She couldn't believe Dominic had said that. The other insults had been obscure to the others, only directed to her. This was a direct thrust, obvious to everyone. If only the boat would sink. She couldn't see her glass clearly now, as tears of shame swam in her eyes. How could Dominic be so cruel to her? Why the need? Just to hurt her, humiliate her before anyone who happened to be near? Doubly hurtful after the words of praise he had spoken only moments before. Why?

The others sat in an uneasy silence, not knowing what to say to such a blatant insult. Bob Driscoll thoughtfully regarded Dominic while Sam and Judy exchanged questioning looks.

'Er, Dominic, I heard you typing the last couple of days. You a writer?' Sam asked, breaking some of the tension.

Dominic lifted his gaze off Lexy's downcast head and turned to Sam, sitting back in his chair, relaxed and seemingly at ease. 'Trying to be. I'm writing something on mines, now. You know anything about mines?'

Sam shook his head, 'Don't think I do. I always thought it would be great to be a writer. Sit around all day, write when you feel like it, be off when you wanted.'

Dominic smiled. 'Not really. There's a long lapse between getting a publisher's nod and the actual publication date of a book. I'd starve if I didn't stick to a strict schedule, and deliver more or less on a regular basis.'

Bob asked if he had written any books before.

'Yes, I have one or two published.'

'Sorry, I haven't read any of your books. Dominic Frazer, no, don't think I've come across any. Publish in America?'

'For heaven's sake, Bob, you wouldn't read a book on mines if it were on the best-seller list,' Judy put in with sisterly candor. She smiled at Dominic. 'I must confess, I've always thought of writers the same way as Sam, but I guess in the end it's plain hard work like anything else.'

'Compensations, though,' Bob put in, 'if you get to write in a locale such as this. Take time out to swim or sail when you want a change.'

'I don't know,' Judy put in. 'Nice, yes, but no parties, no nightclubs, no shows. Must get boring.'

Dominic slanted a glance at Lexy. 'Not boring,' he stated. 'And you're right, Bob, I like it here. When I want to party or socialize, it's a short enough sail to an inhabited island. And there are compensations, even here.' He raised his glass to Bob. 'People stopping by.'

'Nice of you to say so, nice of you to say so.'

'Are you folks on holiday? Traveling around?' Dominic asked.

Bob sat back and told them of his traveling, strictly under doctor's orders. He hated leaving things to his managers, but supposed the fools would manage without him for a few weeks. Judy persuaded him that a cruise in the West Indies would be best, especially if she and Sam were to accompany him, for companionship, and so they had. They had been five weeks now, would probably continue four or five more, then head home for Miami.

The boat was his in Florida, where he used it to cruise the Keys, but he was real pleased with the way she handled in the more open sea and they'd had no difficulties at all.

Lexy gradually relaxed under the storytelling by Bob. He explained things in a quaint southern way and while his drawl sounded odd to Lexy's English ears, she knew exactly what he was saying and found the manner of speech endearing.

By the time he finished, she'd regained enough composure to face the others shyly, yet couldn't bear to meet Dominic's eye.

Judy took up the tale with experiences in the various cities and towns they had visited. Sam groaned and added that his wife thought the sole purpose for her being on the trip was to boost the economy of every island she visited by buying them out. Everyone laughed at this.

'Refills, everyone?' Bob took glasses and, with Sam's help, refilled them.

'Where are you from, Dominic?' Judy asked.

'England, originally. Raised in Barbados, though. Most of my family's here in the Indies.'

'Ever been back?'

'Once, right after I quit school. Cold, I thought.' Again, everyone laughed.

'And you, Lexy, are you from the Indies?' Judy asked gently.

'No, England, though I've been out here a number of years.'

'Did your family move here?' Sam asked.

Lexy flicked an uncertain glance at Dominic, and saw with a thrill of shock the hard glitter of his eyes. 'No, I have no family,' she replied looking away. 'There's only me.'

It was growing quite dark, and the evening had cooled down pleasantly. Bob got up and switched on his anchor light and the dim cockpit lights. They cast a warm glow on the aft deck, giving it a romantic touch.

'Put on some music, Bob,' Judy suggested. 'He has a nice portable player and we brought lots of CD's. It is real pleasant to listen to music, especially on such a grand evening like tonight.'

When Bob brought out the player, Judy turned to Dominic. 'We could dance. It'd be a real party, how about it? With me and Lexy, we could trade off and take turns.'

'Count me out,' Bob said, 'you young people go ahead. I just want to sit and listen to the music.'

'Can't let a compliment like that pass,' Sam said heartily. 'Come on, my love. Dominic, you dance the first one with Lexy.'

Bob started a slow ballad as Sam drew Judy up from her chair. Dominic accepted the invitation, pulling a resistant Lexy into his arms as Sam took Judy, and Bob watched smiling from the deserted table.

Dominic drew her tightly against him, one hand holding hers up, the other on her back, moving slowly, caressing her, rubbing gently up and down. He went beneath her cotton shirt, his fingers warm against the soft bareness of her skin. Rubbing gently up and down, ignoring her attempts to hold herself aloof, apart, straining to pull back from him. He leaned his head against her hair, and slowly they circled the deck. Lexy swayed lightly to the music, disturbed by Dominic's touch, trying to hold back, yet enticed to continue dancing, his touch a mixed delight to her. If only he meant it, if only they could begin again. But his cutting comment earlier put paid to those dreams. They would never progress from where they were. And she ached with the thought.

His fingers found, fumbled, and released her bra fastener, pushing it aside.

'Stop it,' she hissed, drawing back.

'I have,' he murmured, his hand all over her back now. Up to her shoulders, down her spine to her jeans, fingers slipping beneath the tight cloth and then back up again. Her skin soft, warm. His arm still holding her captive, he released her hand to put his other hand around to her back, his hands sensuous against her sensitive skin.

'Fasten me up,' she whispered, glaring at him in the dim lights, still swaying to the soft music, conscious of his body against hers, conscious of the rising excitement in her as his hands continued their wanderings.

'Sure,' he chuckled gently in her ear, leaning over to whisper softly against her hair, 'How Bob and Sam would love that—stop right in the middle of a dance, turn you around and pull your shirt up to search for the straps to fasten up your bra.' He ignored her, moving his hands again, around the side of her ribs and back to her spine. He was tormenting her. She was losing control of her legs, swaying against him, weakening and giving in. He must stop it, it was unfair and he knew it.

'Damn you, Dominic, don't do this.' Lexy was agonized with the feelings his fingers were causing her. Would he never stop? His hands on her back were torment. He knew what he was doing, the reaction he was causing. She pressed against him. 'Stop, Dominic,' she pleaded.

He ignored her protest, dropping a kiss on her hair, 'Shall this be the night I make love to you, Lexy?' he softly asked, whimsically. 'Shall we go back. I'll take off your shirt and mine and have our bare skins against each other.'

'No,' she whispered, close to tears. 'Why do you hurt me all the time?'

'Shall I caress you, fondle you, kiss you; your mouth, your throat, your small breasts. I've never held your breasts, Lexy, will they fill the palms of my hands, will they be firm and taut against my fingers? Your skin, soft and supple. How do you taste, Lexy love, are you as sweet as you smell?'

'Please, stop, oh, Dom, stop!' she begged, pressing against

him. She was almost in tears. The words a torture to her senses. How she would love to have him carry out his plan, to feel his mouth against hers, hard and probing, evoking feelings she yearned for, craved. Feeling his hands on her skin arousing her to the highest delights. His mouth on her breasts, teasing, kissing. Oh, she shuddered against him. She couldn't endure it because he didn't mean a word of it. If he made love to her it would only be to score off points. Something to tell his cousin when he returned to Bridgetown. No real affection or caring behind it on his part. But oh how she wished there were…

'Lexy?' Dominic stopped dancing, both his hands still on her back. He lowered his face, seeking her lips. They opened to receive him, softly pliant to his, responding pressure for pressure, touch for touch. She was lost, she knew it. There was only Dominic, his mouth, his hands, his body.

The sound of the others talking brought them back. Bob was chuckling at something Judy was saying. She and Sam returned to the table, the dance over. Slowly Dominic released her, reluctantly bringing his hands out from her shirt.

'Do yourself up,' he commanded tersely. 'I'll block you.'

They returned to the table, Dominic as if nothing had happened, Lexy almost in tears. How could he be so cool, so controlled? She glared at him. How dared he be unaffected, when her own senses were spinning, her thoughts chaotic! The others looked at each other in puzzlement. On the floor their guests had danced like lovers, yet only a short time ago he had insulted her before all of them. What was their relationship?

On the ride back to the boat some time later, Dominic broke the stillness of the night by mocking her. 'I won't come to you tonight, Lexy, but when I do you'll be ready for me.'

'Never.' She was firm.

'Oh, yes, darling. I felt your responses tonight. When I

come, you'll welcome me with open arms. Continence must be wearing.'

She stiffened at the insult. She would not give in. She was aware her responses tonight had misled him, so that he believed she was the tramp his cousin had denounced. She would be on guard in the future, watch that she did not get caught in a similar situation. She doubted her will power where he was concerned, but had no intention of permitting him to make love to her as if it were his right, as if the lies of Joey Compton were true and she expected it.

'Leave me alone,' she cried.

Dominic chuckled, and continued rowing.

7

The cruiser left the lagoon the next morning, amid horn blowing and friendly waves of farewell. Lexy watched them go, then shook off some of her gloom and went swimming. She did not refer to the small gathering, but was sick at heart for Dominic's cruel cut about her reputation. He not only believed his cousin, he didn't want anyone else to have a good opinion about Lexy Kent, either, if he could help it. She wondered he didn't make her wear a scarlet S for slut, but would not put it past him if she gave him the idea.

She kept telling herself she could not be in love with a man who was so cruel to her, who had such a low opinion of her, but to no avail. She cherished each kind look, each friendly word, fluctuating in hope that he would come to love her and despair that he would forever think of her as the type of woman Joey Compton had said she was.

The next two weeks passed much as the first few days had. Lexy swam, read and kept to herself. Dominic worked hard on his book, spending little time away from his computer, the stack of printed pages growing steadily. Meal times alternated between tentative friendship and cold condemnation. Lexy dreaded their encounters more and more, never knowing whether he would be kind and reasonable, or curt and unforgiving. She ate less and less and started losing weight.

She began having trouble sleeping at night. Dominic's

taunts and barbed phrases coming to mind again and again, ringing in her ears as she tossed and turned restlessly. Finally, unable to stand another night of long lonely hours listening to the echoes of his condemnation, she crept into the head while he was still on deck and found the bottle of sleeping pills Dominic had used when she'd been sick.

Distastefully, Lexy surveyed the small white oval she shook into her hand. She had never had much time for people who used drugs, had never thought she would find a need. Still, for a night or two it couldn't hurt. Once she had a few nights of solid rest behind her she'd feel better. Ordinarily, especially crewing on a boat, she'd never consider such an action. But there was no call to remain alert during the night while anchored in the lagoon. They did not stand watches through the dark; there were no irregular hours to plan for. Lexy popped the pill quickly into her mouth and washed it down with water. At least she'd sleep through tonight.

And the next.

She started taking one pill each night to ensure escape from her thoughts, escape from the memory of Dominic's cold blue eyes; the sound of Joey's accusing voice. What she would do when the supply ran out, she didn't know. For the time being she craved the oblivion sleep brought, knowing each morning it would only be a few long hours until she could once again escape. Could once again forget it all in sleep.

'Lexy, Lexy, wake up!' Dominic was shaking her shoulders, slapping her lightly on her cheeks.

'Go 'way,' she mumbled fathoms deep in sleep, irritated by his shaking.

'Wake up, girl, for God's sake you're a heavy sleeper. Wake

up.' He pulled her upright in the bed, shaking her again.

Slowly Lexy opened her eyes and tried to focus. He was swaying before her, dressed in jeans and a yellow slicker, his head wet. Dully Lexy came awake, she still felt the drag of the sleeping drug, but the effects were less severe now. It was still dark, only the dim light on the bulkhead illuminating the cabin. She blinked and looked around. The sloop was rising and falling, hitting the trough with a crash. The bow caught a wave off center and the sturdy boat sluiced sideways, twisting, corkscrewing in the heavy seas. She looked at Dominic, trying to understand what was happening, trying to break through the heavy fog in her mind. Her head ached a little, and her mouth and throat were dry. She ran her tongue over her lips, and blinked again.

'Lexy, are you awake now?' He shook her again.

'Yes, I'm awake,' she said carefully, shaking her head to clear it. 'What's wrong? What's the matter?' She frowned, holding her stomach, as the Marybeth seemed to fall away beneath her, smacking hard against the water.

'A squall's sprung up. Get dressed and come topside. I want to lash the boom to stop its swing, and try to fix the dinghy. I need your help. Hurry up!' He shook her again, then, satisfied she was awake, shook his head wonderingly. 'I don't know how you got up for your watch before–you sleep heavy.' He turned to leave. 'There's foul-weather gear in the locker by the steps.'

Lexy nodded, already rummaging around for a pair of old jeans. She thrust them on, stuffing her nightshirt in. She felt around for her sneakers, pulling them on without to-do, lacing them tightly. Her fingers felt numb and were slow to respond. Grimly she forced them on; blinking again, shaking her head again and again to keep the clouds of sleep at bay, the boat's wild gyrating making her uncoordinated movements that much more difficult. Finally she was ready.

She staggered out to the main cabin, her own stumbling hindered by the tossing of the sloop. Twice she fell to her knees, finally guiding herself along with her hand on the bulkhead, the sink, the table. She snatched a serviceable yellow slicker and donned it, pushing on the cabin door.

The severe corkscrewing of the vessel should have prepared her, but her drug-dulled mind had not taken in the magnitude of the storm. The door was grabbed from her hands and flung back against the cabin wall by the wind. There was water everywhere, waves splashing over the edge of the deck, the heavens opened with a deluge. Wrestling with the door, Lexy managed to get it shut and latched. It was like being in a pit, a dark, wet, lurching pit.

'Dominic?' she called, afraid he wouldn't hear her above the howl of the wind. Gone was the placid, blue lagoon, surrounded by a solitary beach and magnificent palms. They were in a raging tempest, the sea a boiling, frothing caldron. Carefully she stepped around to the side, holding firmly on to the handrail, the cabin between her and the wind, affording an illusion of safety. The deck, coated with water, was slippery and treacherous. She had no desire for a swim that night. Rounding the corner, she peered into the inky blackness. The only light came from the anchor light and the soft pools spilling out from the cabin lights she had left on.

'Dominic?'

'Yes, come on and hold this line.' When she reached him, he thrust the nylon rope into her fumbling hand. 'Hold it and when I get on the other side, play it out until the boom's centered. Then tie it to the cleat.'

She nodded dumbly, awed by the power of the storm. If it were this bad in the semi-sheltered lagoon, what must it be like on the open sea? Her hair was wet already and a small trickle of water ran down her back beneath the slicker. Her shoes and lower trouser legs were already soaked. She shivered a little, becoming more awake.

'Okay.' Dominic's voice seemed to come from a great distance, the wind snatching it and tossing it away. Slowly she played out the line till she could make out the boom and its position. The boat shuddered and sank in a deep trough, turned now, taking the waves broadside. Wallowing sluggishly, she climbed the next wave. Lexy looked around. The boom was set, she fastened her line, her fingers fumbling a little, but responding to her will in the end.

Another dip. She clutched the handrail, feeling her stomach drop again. Slowly she made her way aft, cautiously treading on the wet deck. The waves were high. She looked to where she thought the shore was, but could see nothing in the inky darkness. Dully, beyond the opposite side of the boat, she heard a dull roar. Looking over she could make out a white line of frothy phosphorescence. Breakers! The waves were large enough in the lagoon now to give surf at the beach. She looked again. They were closer! Wildly Lexy looked around, another trough, the Marybeth fell in it heeling over to port, returning toward starboard as she rose on the next wave.

A touch of fear coursed through Lexy, the anchor had slipped. They were drifting free, and directly towards the beach!

'Dominic!' she screamed. 'Dominic!'

He appeared at once, passing her and going to the wheel. She caught up with him. 'The anchor's not holding,' she yelled above the cacophony of the storm. 'We're drifting.'

'I know, I realized it when we turned to broadside, at anchor we would have stayed bow into the wind.' He seemed remarkably calm about the situation, Lexy thought with a touch of hysteria. She looked to the surf again, it was definitely closer.

She drew a deep breath; all thoughts of sleep finally dispelled, fear under control.

'What do you want me to do?' she yelled.

'I'll start the engine and turn her about, stand by to haul in the anchor, I don't want the line fouling the propeller.'

'The dinghy?'

'I cut that line.' He went to the cabin. 'I'll get the key.' Minutes later Dominic turned the ignition on the engine.

Nothing happened. He switched it off, pumped the intake clear and tried again. A soft whirring, then nothing. Lexy licked her lips, judging the distance to the shore now. They were close, very close. How steeply did it shelve off? She tried to remember. The deep keel of the sailboat made it dangerous to get too close. If the keel hit, held the boat to the mercies of the pounding waves, it could destroy the Marybeth. Idly she wondered how long it might be before another pleasure boat found the lagoon and found the survivors of a capsized sloop.

'Damn battery is low.' Dominic straightened. 'Turn off the cabin lights and the anchor light, then reel in the anchor.'

Lexy whirled to do his bidding. With the lights gone, it was a nightmare. The sea gives off little light at night. Lexy felt her way forward, her heart pounding, her mind achingly aware of the precious seconds ticking away while the sea carried the Marybeth closer and closer to destruction. Please let the engine start she prayed. How much more so must Dominic want it to start, the Marybeth was his home. She found the winch for the anchor by stumbling into it. She wedged herself as best she could on the deck and began cranking. It didn't take her long, the anchor dragged freely along the coral bed of the lagoon. She almost cried with relief, with thanksgiving, when she felt the comforting throb of the engine beneath her feet. Slowly the bow came around, the wild dipping stopped. They were headed into the wind, leaving the shore behind.

The winch refused to wind further. She ventured to the edge, holding on tightly against the rise and dip of the bow, and peered out. Was that black splotch the anchor nesting against the side of the ship? She wiggled back. She hoped it was, impossible to tell without more light, but she hoped it was.

The walk back to the helm would have done credit to any amusement park specializing in thrill rides. The boat continued its see-saw action, now dipping beneath the crest of a wave, water cascading along the deck, sweeping ahead of Lexy, then receding, only to come again one or two waves later. Her hands ached from grasping the safety rail, but twice her feet slipped and only that rail saved her from an untimely swim.

When Lexy reached the edge of the cabin she timed the rise and fall of the sloop, moving towards the helm on a bow rise and cannoning into Dominic to stop her headlong rush.

'Whee,' she said gaily, giddy with relief. 'Nice evening you drummed up. What was wrong with peaceful stillness?'

He smiled, his teeth flashing in the night. 'Variety is the spice of life, my girl. Anchor secure?'

'Yes.' She stumbled against the seesaw action.

Dominic reached over for her, pulling her before him, between his outstretched arms. His hands firm on the wheel, his arms and body caging her, holding her against the ravages of the ship.

Lexy put her hands on the wheel, to help keep her balance, help her resist falling back against his strong chest. She felt safe at last.

'I think we're all right now,' he rumbled in her ear.

'Will you take her out of the lagoon?' she called back, comforted and feeling secure.

'Are you crazy? If the lagoon's like this, think of the open sea. No, I just want enough power to keep her bow into the wind, and a few good yards between us and the beach.'

'Is it a hurricane?' she asked after a while. She really didn't care, as long as she could stay sheltered in his arms for a little while longer, could pretend he cared for her, was protecting her.

'No, wrong season. Just a nice little tropical storm. Should blow out by morning.'

So it proved. By the time the first gray streaks appeared in the sky, the wind was lessening. Dawn came dully, heavy clouds blocking the sun, lumbering across the sky. The light was a welcomed change, the stronger it grew, the less tempestuous the sea. By eight o'clock, the wind was only a soft breeze, the lagoon again a sheltered stretch of water, the large swells the only sign of the violence of the night.

'I'll try the anchor again,' Dominic said, rousing at last. 'Hold us on course, then when I drop it, cut the engine to idle. If she doesn't hold, I'll signal you.'

'Okay.' Lexy felt oddly bereft when he stepped away. For hours they had stood as one in the storm. Not talking, just sharing the tempest quietly, riding it out together. She had felt protected, almost cosseted. Now it was over. Back to pistols at dawn, she muttered, watching for his signal, cutting back the engine.

'We're set,' Dominic called.

She shut off the engine completely and slowly headed for the cabin. She could use a strong cup of tea, and knew Dominic could, too. She stopped short when opening the door, appalled by the devastation that met her eyes.

'Oh, no!'

'What now?' Dominic looked over her shoulder. Every paper, every note, every pencil and pen had flown from the table during the tossing storm and was scattered hither and thither on the cabin floor. In the middle of the mess was the laptop, upside down on the floor.

He pushed passed her and went carefully down the steep stairs, picking up papers as he went. 'Could be worse, could have gotten water on them.'

'That's true,' she agreed, starting to help. Very little actual harm was done, after all. Only a few hours' work, and the stacks would be sorted again. She picked up a handful of the printed pages, turning them so they were all right side up, putting them in numerical order.

'Damn!'

She looked up. Dominic had placed the laptop on the table and was now tapping the keys.

'Broken?' she hazarded.

'Yes.'

'Can you fix it?'

'No, I can't.'

Compassionately she averted her eyes. What a disappointment. They would have to go somewhere to have it repaired and it would delay him a few days, if not longer. Still, after the terrible storm, to have the only damage be to the laptop was a lucky stroke. She glanced up under her lashes, to see that Dominic was soberly picking up the papers, roughly sorting them, his face shuttered.

They ate a quiet breakfast, tired from the night's exertions, dispirited with the turn of events. Lexy found her eyes on Dominic more and more, wanting to offer encouragement, afraid of his rebuff. Finally she gathered her courage.

'I'm sorry for the delay, Dominic. I know it must be frustrating for you.'

He looked at her, eyes glinting. 'It's not all that bad. You'll have a little civilization, parties and all. It'll take a few days to have new laptop flown in. I printed out everything, but don't know if I can retrieve the data from the hard drive. Time will tell, I suppose.'

She dropped her eyes. 'I don't go to parties,' she said evenly, sipping her tea.

'No need to avoid them now, Lexy. I know all the damning details, or at least all I want to know. You needn't worry someone will drop a clanger now.'

She looked up swiftly at this. 'Is that why you think I didn't stay on at Robin's and Sarah's?' At his nod, she resumed her tea. 'Maybe you're right,' she conceded. 'I don't go because I want to avoid men who get the erroneous idea of what I am and what I will agree to.' She paused, maybe he would listen to her now. 'I really didn't do everything Joey said,' she began.

He raised a stern face, 'No talking about the past, Lexy, we agreed to that.'

She frowned. She didn't remember any agreement, just his dictatorial laying down rules for her keeping the job. She sighed softly. 'Will we be returning to Bridgetown?'

'No. My aunt lives a little south of us on the Island of Santa Theresa. The island's a decent size enough to have a town. I'll use her computer until a new one can be ordered and flow in from Barbados. We'll be there a few days at least. It'll take one day's sail there and one back. I could be delayed a week or two by going to Bridgetown.' He smiled sardonically, 'No escape yet, my lovely Lexy.'

Dominic used the engine to leave the lagoon. The picture prettiness of the setting dimmed by the gray overcast sky, the torn palm fronds and seaweed-covered beach. Dominic had braved the still rough water to swim to the half submerged dinghy, pulling it up on shore to await their return. With it secured, they headed south. Once clear of the lagoon, they hoisted both sails, tacking back and forth to use the wind.

'Take the wheel, Lex,' Dominic said. 'I have to pull the charts and plot our course. Just keep heading south, keep track of how long on each leg.'

She nodded and took over. The wind was gusty, coming from the south, southeast. She steadied the wheel, keeping watch on the billowing sails, white against the gray sky. The seas were heavy now, iron-gray with whitecaps like frothy foam scattered as far as the eye could see.

'Right, I'll take it.' He returned a short time later.

She relinquished the wheel, reporting her directions and times, then casually, 'I'll go below and straighten things. Give a shout if you need me.'

She was anxious not to waste a minute, here was a perfect opportunity to read the new pages of his book. She had put the typewritten stack in order while Dominic was seeing to the dinghy; tempted to read some then, she had been unable to do so in the short time she had. She was impatient to see how the book had been developing over the last two weeks, but Dominic's almost constant working had made that impossible.

She gathered the precious papers, stealing into her cabin and locking the door. Gleefully she sank on the bunk, turning to where she had left off, resuming her surreptitious reading. Soon caught up in the plot, Lexy forgot all time, forgot her surroundings, her still damp jeans. She was laboring in the hot South American jungle, taking the blows of the hero, trying to see a way clear. With great reluctance she reached the last page. How could Dominic stop there? She wished he'd been able to get more done. Who knew when she'd have another chance to read again? She tidied the stack. Maybe two or three pages were still mixed in with his notes. She took the stack of papers and returned them to the table, placing them beside the broken laptop. Rummaging through the yellow foolscap and small scraps of notes, she searched in vain for more typed copy. He had not written anymore.

She straightened his notes, cleaned and wiped down the galley and remade the sofa. According to Dominic they would reach Santa Theresa Island before night and would not need to use the boat for sleeping while they were there.

It was after dark before the lights denoting the small port town were sighted. The day had remained dreary, with a scattered shower or two keeping them wet and cold. The wind against them slowed down their travel, as they had to go twice the distance, tacking back and forth as necessary.

Dominic skimmed past the cluster of lights, which was the town and sailed around a promontory. A small group of lights glowed in the dark. Starting the engines, dropping their sails and several toots on the horn prepared them for docking. All at once a string of lights went on, illuminating a private pier, extending into the sea.

'Almost there,' Dominic said, maneuvering the sloop towards the light.

'Dominic,' a thought just occurred to Lexy. 'This aunt of yours isn't Joey's mother, is she?' Please, not that.

'No, Aunt Patience is my father's sister, his eldest sister. She's never married. You'll see her soon, if I know her. She'll be on the dock awaiting us.' He glanced around at Lexy, his face softening slightly. 'You'll like her, she's forthright, but kind.'

Lexy almost shouted her relief. She gave Dominic a shy smile, her heart swelling with the almost kind look he was giving her.

'I'll get my stuff for tonight,' she mumbled, turning towards the cabin. If there was a reception committee on the dock, now would be the best time to get the precious sleeping pills, it might be impossible later, and Lexy didn't want to chance lying awake this night or the next because of her thoughts.

8

Patience Frazer was awaiting their arrival on her dock; a tall woman, thin, with short iron-gray hair and the blue eyes Dominic's father had passed on to him. She greeted her nephew with open arms, booming his welcome from the top of her lungs.

'Lord love us, Dom, it's been an age. Glad you've come my boy, glad to see you again.'

He swept her up into a big hug as soon as she dropped on board. Lexy was touched at his overt display of affection. The tall woman was flushed and beaming when he set her on her feet again.

'Well, let me look at you. You've lost a little weight. You need a wife to watch out for you. You work too hard on those danged books.'

Dominic chuckled. 'Those danged books give me food to eat and a place to lay my head.'

'No need for this fancy boat to lay your head, you are always welcomed to a bedroom in my place.'

'To be plagued by everybody who drops by your house. You are the most popular person on the island—I'd never get anything done!'

'Why are you here, then?' she boomed again.

'We ran into a storm, rather one ran into us. Broke my computer. I need to get another before I can head out again. And see if Simon can get the data off my hard drive.'

'Humph,' she sniffed. 'Who's this with you. Not Robin, if I know Sarah.'

Dominic laughed again, an almost boyish look to him. 'You're right. I hired on a crewman to take Robin's place. Lexy?' He spotted her standing quietly by the cabin door, silent and still. 'Come and meet Aunt Patience.'

Lexy stepped forward and offered her hand. 'How do you do?' she said softly.

Patience Frazer stared at her, dumbfounded. Finding her wits at last she took the younger woman's hand pumping it up and down.

'Howdy do? Well, aren't you a pretty sight. This is your crewman, Dominic?' She stared in disbelief first at Lexy, then Dominic.

'Yes,' Dominic replied curtly. 'Alexis Kent, my aunt Patience Frazer, but don't let the name fool you, she should have been called Impatience.'

'That's enough out of you, young man. Alexis Kent, Lexy, he called you?'

'That's my nickname.'

'Well, welcome to Land's End, not too original, but I like it,' Patience boomed out, a broad grin covering her face. 'Welcome, welcome.' She turned to Dominic, her eyes twinkling, 'Come away in, it's getting late.'

Patience Frazer led the way from the pier, up the flagstone pathway to a large two-storied villa. Lights spilled out from the long windows on the ground floor, picking up some of the bright colors in the tubs of flowers surrounding the veranda. The entryway was open and cool, offering a choice of doors, with a curving staircase leading to the second floor.

'Did you eat dinner yet?' Patience asked, leading the way into a comfortable open great room. French doors lined one wall,

open to the evening breeze, the bare terrazzo floors, polished
and cool. It was minimally furnished, but the pieces were large
and comfortable—an oversized sofa, several easy chairs, and,
unexpectedly, a stone fireplace along one wall. Lexy's gaze was
immediately drawn to it.

'Didn't expect to see one of those here, ha!' Patience laughed
at Lexy's surprise. 'I like a fire, always have, insisted on that when
I had the place built. Use it some when I can. Not often, it's too
danged hot for it. Once in a while we get a night cool enough
for one. What'll you have?'

Lexy looked surprised, darting a questioning glance at
Dominic. Patience Frazer noticed the look but said nothing.

'A nightcap, Lexy, would you like one?' Dominic answered
her masked question.

'No, thank you. A cup of tea, maybe,' she said hesitantly.

'Sit down, sit down.' Patience waved her to the sofa and
turned to her nephew. 'Go see if Molly's still up and ask her to
fix a pot of tea. Then bring the brandy, you know where it's kept.'
She waved him from the room, quick to pick up his reluctant
glance at Lexy and hers to him, again making no comment.
Patience sat in one of the chairs and fixed her eye on Lexy.

'You two lovers?' she boomed out, surprising her new guest.

Lexy's eyes widened at the unexpected attack, then she drew
a shaky breath. 'No,' she replied composedly. Good grief, what
would Dominic say. She stifled a giggle.

'Why not?' It was Patience's turn to look surprised.
'Something is wrong with the two of you then. He's a fine man
and you're a right pretty gal. What with the morals like they are
these days, I'm surprised, downright surprised.'

Lexy smiled, answering in her soft musical voice, 'He just
hired me for his crew, since Robin won't be going any more.'

'You met Robin?' Patience asked sharply.

'Oh, yes. I stayed one night at his house. Sarah and Robin are both delightful people. I had a lovely time.'

'Dominic there, too?'

'Yes, he's the one who invited me. We, er, I had crewed for him from Santa Inez to Barbados and as we were sailing again for the little island, he invited me to stay with them while in Bridgetown. I think he worried about me on the boat alone at night.' She fell silent, remembering how things had been between the two of them then. He certainly wouldn't worry about her again, nor invite her to his brother's a second time.

Patience looked thoughtful. Watching Lexy curiously, but not saying anything further, rousing herself only when she heard Dominic returning. He carried the brandy decanter and three brandy glasses. Placing them all on the table before the sofa he sat down beside Lexy, leaning back on the soft cushions, his legs stretched out before him. Lexy watched him nervously from the corner of her eye.

'I brought three glasses in case Lexy changes her mind and wants to join us,' he said as Patience poured some of the amber liquid into two glasses. She hesitated over the third, looking inquiringly at Lexy.

'No, really, thanks. I'll just have the tea.'

'Molly up?' Patience handed Dominic his glass.

'Yes, she'll bring the tea in when it's ready.'

'Are you from the West Indies, Lexy?' Patience asked.

Lexy's eyes again sought Dominic, aware he was watching her lazily, awaiting her reply to his aunt's question. She hesitated, unwilling to answer something he could twist or turn against her. She licked her lips nervously, disconcerted by the faintly sardonic smile on Dominic's face as he watched her.

'I'm from England, originally,' she answered at last, her eyes wide and appealing on Dominic's. He raised an eyebrow at the brief answer, but remained silent, sipping his brandy and watching her over the rim.

Patience could feel the rising tension between the two of them and was puzzled by it. What did it mean? She was not the type to be put off by a mystery. Before they left she'd find out, or make a good try.

'I'm originally from England. Came out when Dom's father got a job out here. Never regretted it. Don't like the cold, never did. You come out with your family?'

Before Lexy could reply a large black woman came wheezing in carrying a heavy tea tray, her bare feet slapping softly on the bare floor.

'Here's the tea. This little girl the one having it? It'll fix you right up, miss.' She plopped the tray down, rattling the cup and saucer, splashing a drop or two from the spout as she poured hot fragrant tea into the cup. 'You drink that while's hot.' She beamed down at Lexy, gave Dominic a big wink.

'I done made the beds fresh, Miss Patience, everything set for the visitors. I'm going to bed now. See you fine folks in the morning. Mind you drink the tea while's hot.' She shuffled from the room closing the door behind her.

Lexy wished she could go with her, escape the questioning from Dominic's aunt, escape his presence, ready to pounce on her as soon as he tired of playing with her emotions, as soon as she thought she was safe and could relax.

She rubbed her fingers shakily across her forehead. She wished she could go to bed now. The pills were in her bag, in only a few minutes she could be oblivious to it all. She drank her tea, the china cup clacking slightly against her teeth. As soon as she could, she would plead tiredness and retire.

'You didn't tell me if you came to the West Indies with your family,' Patience reminded her gently, watching with great interest as Lexy took a deep breath, her eyes flickering to Dominic again before replying.

'I worked my passage over, actually. I wanted to see the world. You're right about the cold, I don't think I'd like to live in England again.'

Dominic watched her enigmatically. She licked her lips and took a sip of the tea. It was hot.

'You're very adventuresome, working your way here. Then did you hire on with Dominic? I confess I'm interested in knowing how you got the job.'

'Actually, I've held several positions since I came to the Caribbean. I was between jobs when I saw his notice and applied.'

'And it turns out we, we discovered we had mutual friends,' Dominic drawled. 'Joey Compton.'

Patience could see the blow hit home as Lexy visibly flinched and dropped her eyes to her tea. Patience regarded her nephew, narrowing her eyes, curious as to why that simple statement should cause such a reaction from the girl's face.

'Tell Aunt Patience about your jobs,' he invited, still watching Lexy lazily, aware of the effect he was having on her.

'Stop it,' she hissed, glaring at him.

'Lexy, love,' he feigned surprise, 'whatever is the matter?'

She glanced apologetically to Patience. 'I worked for a marine biologist for several years, when I first came to the Indies.'

'Miles Jackson,' Dominic interposed helpfully.

'That's where I learned to sail. Then I worked for a photographer, and . . .'

'Which one was he?' Dominic asked sotto voce.

'... A businessman, and an American couple living on Santa Inez.'

Patience nodded, interested. 'A nice variety, you must be older than you look. It's good to be well rounded, and a variety of experience can come in helpful.'

'I agree, Aunt Patience. Tell us about your other experiences, Lexy, your work in England,' he said, studying her averted face. 'Tell us Lexy, we want to know.'

She turned to him, bitterness and despair ravaging her face, her eyes enormous in the artificial light. Before she could speak, however, Patience cut in ruthlessly.

'What I want to know is how your book is coming on?' she demanded, meeting her nephew's gaze with compelling eyes. He bowed his head in temporary surrender, aware of his aunt's tactics.

'It's coming all right, ask Lexy, she's read it.' He leaned back against the soft cushions, studying his brandy, ignoring the consternation around him.

It would be difficult to say who was more astonished, though for different reasons, Lexy or Patience. In a night full of surprises and undercurrents, this one crowned them all.

Patience looked at Lexy, perplexity clearly defined. 'You've read Dominic's manuscript?'

Lexy looked in amazement at Dominic, scarcely aware of Patience's question. He was looking casually at his glass, unconcerned, certainly not blazing angry. She licked her lips. How did he know? How had he found out?

'Lexy,' Patience tried again, louder this time, 'you have read his manuscript? Is it finished?'

Lexy shook her head, unsure how to answer. 'No, it is not finished, but I can hardly wait for it to be finished. I think it is the best he's done. I have all his other books and this one is as good, no, better than any of the others,' she ended in a rush, happy to be able to put into words what she felt about his manuscript.

Dominic smiled and looked up to meet her eyes. 'But then you are biased, my love,' he said lightly. Her heart skipped a beat at the taunting endearment. If only he meant it. If only it could be true.

'I didn't know you knew. That I'd read it, I mean. I thought you'd be angry.'

'And so I should be! I distinctly told you that you could not read it.'

She shrugged helplessly. 'I know, but I had to see it. I can't wait for you to finish it, I'm dying to see how Morgan–'

'Shh!' He held up his hand and nodded to his aunt. 'You can read the rest when I'm finished, but absolutely no talking about it.'

Patience widened her eyes as sheer incredulity showed. 'Tomorrow morning we will have to have a nice private chat, Miss Lexy Kent,' she said with a sly look at Dominic. 'In all the years Dominic has been writing, no one—aunt, brother, or friend—has seen his manuscripts. Only when the books were published could we see what he had written. This news is almost too much to bear!'

Dominic chuckled appreciatively.

'But,' Patience continued, 'it's getting late, now. I suggest we retire until morning. Dominic, you have your own room. Lexy, I've put you in across from me. Come on now. Got something to sleep in?'

Lexy nodded and stood; glad to be able to end the evening. Maybe tomorrow she could go for a long walk and stay out of everybody's way—by that she meant Dominic. She wanted some time completely free of the fear of another insult, another taunt. She also did not wish to be questioned extensively by Dominic's aunt. She shook her head slightly, this might prove to be more difficult than being alone with him on the island.

Patience led the way up the lovely curved staircase, and stopped at the top.

'Goodnight, Dom, sleep well. I hope you will, not being on the boat and all. Lexy, too.'

'I will, Aunt Patience.' He kissed her cheek. 'Lexy will too, she always does, but not necessarily alone.' He quirked a look at the target of his barb, but she refused to meet his eye.

'Come on, my dear, our rooms are down this way.' Patience led the way to the right, opening a door partway down, snicking on the light. It was pleasantly furnished in French provincial, a pink coverlet on the bed, matching soft pink pillows piled at the head, frothy pink curtains billowed at the windows.

'Sleep well, my dear. Lie in as long as you want tomorrow. I wake early myself, but the old don't need a lot of sleep. Bathroom's through there.' She pointed out a door to the left of the bed.

'Thank you, Patience, you're most accommodating. I'm sure I'll be fine. Goodnight.'

Lexy wasted no time getting ready for bed. In the morning she'd take full advantage of the tub and have a long soak. Tonight she just wanted to sleep. When she was dressed for bed, she dug the pills from her purse. Greedily she gulped one down, swallowing the water from a small cup from the bathroom. The bottle dropped to the bedside table, tomorrow she would put it back in her purse, in the morning.

The waves began washing over her, relaxing her, putting her beyond all hurt and taunts of Dominic. Vaguely through the clouds of sleep she thought she heard her door open, felt a small stir of fresh air, as if someone had raised her window a little, but too near the edge of sleep, she was too tired to raise her eyes, and she slept.

The next thing Lexy knew hard, angry fingers had yanked

her up and were shaking and shaking her. She came awake suddenly, dazed as to where she was, what was happening. 'Oh, stop. What is it? Stop! You are hurting me.'

Dominic's angry face swam into focus. He was furious and shaking her as if she were to blame.

'I should have known the other night when it was so hard to wake you up.' He shook her again, her head bobbing helpless on her slender neck.

'Ow! Dominic, what's wrong? Stop, you're hurting me!'

He pushed her back against her pillows, breathing hard as he shoved her legs aside and sat hard on the edge of the bed.

'I ought to do more than that. How long have you been using these?' He reached out for the bottle beside the bed. 'Damn, they're mine!' he exclaimed, reading the label.

'They are not,' she defended stoutly. 'They're for a Dave Sullivan.'

'Don't quibble; these are the ones you got from the boat. How long have you been taking them?'

Lexy licked her lips, they were always so dry in the morning when she used the pills, her mouth and throat too. 'A couple of weeks,' she said at last.

'You didn't need them last night, you must have been dead on your feet. We were up from about three in the morning and I know you didn't take a nap, you were reading the damn book.'

She gratefully seized upon this. 'I did, how did you know that's when I read it?'

'I went down for something to drink. You were forward, with the door closed, and the pile of papers gone. Doesn't take much genius to figure that out.' He studied the bottle absently, twirling it around in his fingers. 'It wasn't the first time, either, was it, that you read what I'd written?'

'No, I read it one afternoon when you went ashore to the

island, but I thought I replaced the papers just like you had them.'

'You almost did. Something made me wonder, and I knew when I told Bob Driscoll I was writing about mines—I could feel your reaction.

'I'm sorry I went behind your back. My curiosity was so strong; I couldn't resist the first time. Then I've been dying to read more ever since. It is good, Dominic. Yesterday was the first time I had another opportunity.

He was silent, his face unreadable.

'I didn't gush. No, I loved it but–, No, Don't you think–''' she teased him softly, remembering his reasons for not sharing his work before.

He turned, eyebrow raised. 'Not voiced them, perhaps, but then you often display remarkable self-discipline.'

She drew her knees up, conscious of his nearness, his presence in her bedroom. Not that she need worry, her sleeping attire was quite modest, if he should even notice.

'I would say it was wonderful. I don't have anything to add,' she replied slowly, sincerely. 'I look forward to reading the rest, but I'll wait until you give it to me,' she promised solemnly. 'I'm sorry I went behind your back.'

'Shall I tell you what's going to happen?'

'No! I want to read it, with all the words you write out, your phrases and descriptions. You'd summarize and finish it in three sentences. I'll wait for the book.' She played with the edge of the sheet. 'I do have one question, though. Did you go to South America and travel through the jungle?' she asked.

He smiled. 'Yes. I spent a few days there for description. I tried my hand at whacking things with a machete to get the exact feel. The rest is pure imagination.'

She smiled at him, watching as his expression changed as he remembered the sleeping pills.

'Does your conscience bother you, Lexy, so much you can't sleep nights, that you have to resort to drugs?'

The mood was shattered, the peaceful interlude destroyed. She bit her lip, looking up at him, 'No, not my conscience, but your insults and tormenting comments. They ring in my ears night after night. I can't sleep, so I take the pills.'

He reached out his hand slowly and drew her up into his arms. 'I don't know about you, Lexy—just when I think I've come to terms with you, something upsets the scales. Are you an innocent caught up by circumstances? Low resistance? Or just very, very clever?'

He lowered his head, slowly kissing her mouth, his hands caressing the softness of her back. The kiss went on and on, endless, sweet, promising. Gently he released her and lowered her back on her pillows. She gazed at him with bemused eyes, half prepared for a cutting remark sure to come now.

'No more drugs, Lexy, or I swear, I will find a way to keep you away from them. Understand?' he said, his voice uncompromising.

She swallowed, nodding her head.

He rose and crossed to the bathroom, flushing the remaining pills down the toilet. When he returned to her room, he leaned against the doorjamb, surveying her recumbent form, the navy-blue shirt a sharp contrast to the light-pink sheets.

'I would have thought your sleepwear would run more along the lines of your underwear,' he drawled, insolently regarding her.

'Oh, get out, Dominic,' she said, rolling over on her side, her back towards him.

He walked across the floor towards the hall door, pausing to say, 'I'm taking my computer in to be looked at, and to order a new one. Do you want anything from town?'

'Town?' she turned back.

'Yes, around the promontory is the town of Santa Theresa, small but fairly modern. You want something?'

'No, I don't need anything.' She watched him leave, an idea taking shape. If there were a town near by, perhaps she could arrange transportation off the island. She didn't care where to at the moment, just away from here, away from insults and humiliation, away from a man she loved so dearly but who considered her a tramp.

It would take a while to get a new computer, he'd said. She should have several days to find out information about ships calling, or any air traffic. She'd go down to the sloop later and pack her things so as to be ready when something presented itself. If only it took a week or longer for the computer, she could be long gone before he was ready to set sail again.

Patience Frazer was sitting at the umbrella table when Lexy came down an hour later, having taken full advantage of the deep tub and fragrant bath salts found in her bathroom. Lexy had finished with a shower, washing her hair and had wished, for the first time in a long time, she had a frilly, feminine dress to wear, instead of her jeans and shirt. Sure, she jeered, as if that would change anything.

She found her way downstairs, drawn outside by the beautiful view offered through the opened French doors. When she spotted her hostess, she strolled over to join her.

Patience Frazer was having her breakfast, as was her custom, at the umbrella-covered table on her front veranda. The villa faced the sea, with the veranda overlooking the sweep of green lawn, and the pier where the Marybeth rode proudly, her dark-blue hull contrasting with the turquoise of the sea, the cabin gleaming white in the early morning sun. Fluffy white puffs dotted the pale blue of the sky. The air was fragrant with the scent of the garden's many flowers. It was still and warm.

Patience smiled a welcome, 'Good morning, Lexy, join me for breakfast. Did you sleep well?'

Lexy blushed a little, remembering the result of her sleeping with the pills and her rude awakening this morning. 'Thank you, I did. Sorry to sleep in so late.'

'No problem. Molly!' She called her cook and ordered breakfast for Lexy, despite the latter's protests a cup of tea would suffice.

'Nonsense, you'll never grow big and strong like me if you don't eat,' Patience boomed in her hearty voice.

'I'm afraid my growing days are over.' Lexy smiled at her hostess.

'Here we are. Thank you, Molly.'

Patience nodded as Lexy began to eat some of the papaya, fresh croissants and pineapple on her dish. True to her name, Patience waited patiently for Lexy to assuage her hunger before opening a conversation. She watched the younger woman, just short of outright staring, only glancing from time to time at the sloop tied to the dock, as if seeking some answers.

'I'm very glad to meet you, Lexy, and to know you and that you've come,' Patience said at last, gently, in a voice Lexy had not heard before.

She looked up in surprise. 'Well, thank you, but why?'

'I think you must be a very special person.'

That answer was a puzzle, and Lexy showed her confusion.

'How long have you known my nephew?'

'About a month,' Lexy replied. Was it only a month since she had applied for the crewing job, full of hopes, dreams?

Patience looked startled, then pleased. 'Only a month, imagine! Lexy, what do you know of Dominic's life before he met you—anything?'

'Very little. I know he used to have Robin crew for him until he married Sarah. He's written thirteen books. I read them before I knew he was Nick Roberts.'

'He was married once, a long time ago.'

'Yes, to Marybeth, he named the sloop for her.'

'She died after they had been married, oh I guess just over a year. He loved her very much. She was tall, blonde. Regal, almost, in looks. And,' Patience paused, fixing Lexy's eyes, 'a perfect ninny. She didn't have a parcel of sense.'

Lexy was shocked.

'You must remember, dear,' Patience continued, 'Dominic was not then the man he is now. He was very young, untried, and blinded by her beauty. Oh, I don't mean to disparage Marybeth. I loved her, too, in my way, but she was not the woman for Dominic. Once the shock wore off from her death, she died of an undetected heart defect, 1 thought maybe it wasn't so bad she'd died so young, he would have outgrown her; or worse, she would have ruined him.'

Lexy's eyes never wavered. She sat forward in her chair, fascinated by this history.

'Dominic was working on his first book when they were married, and it almost was his last attempt. She had no idea he could write so well, couldn't recognize his gift when she saw it, nagged him to stop wasting time and get a real job. Preferably in Bridgetown, where she could attend parties, visit nightclubs, go to the hairdressers, go to the shops. She read some of his work, harping on minor inconsistencies, or calling the plot too far-fetched for anyone to believe it. It was good, but, rather too sexy, rather too violent. On and on.'

Patience paused again, Lexy had closed her eyes—here was Dominic's reason for not sharing his work prior to publication. His own wife. His first book, when he needed all the encouragement and praise he could get to keep him going, keep his doubts minimal, and his own wife couldn't give him that encouragement. Lexy was growing to dislike the fair Marybeth.

'Are you all right?' Patience asked.

'Yes, I was remembering some things Dominic said to me once, I didn't know it was his wife he had been talking about.'

Again Patience wondered about the relationship between her nephew and this young woman.

'Please, go on,' Lexy said.

'Hum? Oh, well, Marybeth died and he swore no one would read a manuscript except his publisher. Not aunt, nor brother, nor close family friend. I must admit I was surprised when I heard he had let you. But then, maybe it's not so surprising. You see, Lexy dear, from Marybeth's death until now, I've not known Dominic to have anything to do with any woman. You, my dear, came as quite a shock to me.'

'But surely...' Lexy stopped.

'Oh, I'm not saying he hasn't had someone on the side now and again. I think Dominic is very much the man. But never to bring home, never to introduce to his family.'

Lexy's shoulders drooped. If only she knew. 'Don't get the wrong impression, Patience. I just crew for him. I think he despises me.'

Patience waited.

'You see,' Lexy continued in the silence, 'I met him in Santa Inez and we sailed to Bridgetown, sort of a trial run, to see how it would work. He was very reluctant to have a female crew for him, yet it seemed to work rather well. We agreed to continue the arrangement while he wrote his book. I was glad of the job, and . . . and liked him. We were several days in Bridgetown, so he had me over to meet Robin and Sarah. We had a lovely time,' she said wistfully, remembering.

Then her eyes darkened with remembered pain. 'Then a mutual acquaintance told Dominic some rather unpleasant gossip about me. Everything changed. From that moment on, everything changed. He wouldn't listen to me, hear my side of the story. But judged and condemned me on hearsay.'

'In Bridgetown, you said?'

'Yes.' She ate some of her pineapple, regretting already her revelation. She wasn't out for any sympathy.

'Can't have mattered too much, you're still with him.'

'Oh, but he didn't find out until late, we were ready to sail. He needed a crew, so I had to go along. It would have delayed him too much to find a new sailor.' Her eyes were bright with unshed tears. 'I know he's regretted it ever since.'

Patience thought back to the scene last night, how her nephew with only a few words could subject Lexy to hurt and pain, almost as if he were compelled to do so.

'Give him some time, if you will, child,' Patience urged her. 'I think, this is my own opinion mind, but I think he somehow feels relieved Marybeth's gone, relieved he can remember her with love and longing, that in his heart he knows they would not suit now. Yet somehow guilty that he is alive and interested in someone else now. It's... it's unchivalrous.'

'And he considers himself a chivalrous man,' Lexy sighed. Poor Patience, so fond of her nephew she would excuse him anything, hoping for his happiness. She would urge anyone to stay if it pleased Dominic, never mind the hell they themselves would have to endure. But Lexy couldn't stay. She wouldn't take any more of his digs, his insults, his condemnation. She bit her lip, unbidden tears rising. She loved him so much, why couldn't he at least be kind to her, so she could have had sweet memories of the man she knew she would always love.

Patience shook her head in disgust as Lexy went off into a

world of her own. She wished she knew what was wrong between the two of them, She wished she could bang their heads together and bring some sense to them. The problem could not be insurmountable, for despite the bad time he was giving Lexy, he had brought her to his family, he had let her read his manuscript, and he was very protective of her.

Patience shook her head, the young made such mountains but of things.

'Lexy, give him more time. He can be very demanding in his ideals. He's such an upright individual himself; he finds it hard to excuse ordinary failings in us mortals. I won't pry as to the gossip, but I'm sure it was unpleasant and he leaped to the conclusion it was true.'

Lexy looked at Patience, nodding her head slowly. 'He won't even give me a chance to explain, to tell him what the circumstances were. Just freezes me off, believing the worst and—and rubbing my face in it all the time.'

Waving her hands dismissively, Patience said airily, 'I've found that always true, people tend to believe the worst. I don't know why really, but time is a great equalizer, and a great revealer. Almost everything comes to light sooner or later, though more often later more's the pity. Well, enough of this philosophizing. Tonight we'll have a party!'

'Oh, no,' Lexy exclaimed involuntarily. She smiled apologetically at her hostess. 'It's just that Sarah did the same thing. Dominic came for a few days and she immediately threw a party. I didn't go.'

'Why not?'

Tracing the rim of her cup with a shapely finger, Lexy's response was low, 'I didn't want to run into old acquaintances. Besides, I have nothing to wear to a party, only jeans and shirts.'

'Oh, that's easily arranged. We'll run into town this

afternoon and pick up a little sundress. That's all you'll need. As to the other, I can almost guarantee you won't meet anyone at my house tonight who you know. Let yourself go, Lexy, and have a little fun. You've been cooped up too long on Dom's island; you need the flattery of other men, the exchange of confidences with girls your own age. I'll help you pick out your dress.'

'Oh, but...'

All of Lexy's excuses and protestations were overruled. Patience would have her way. They didn't see Dominic before they left for the small town of Santa Theresa after lunch. It was a quiet, sleepy little town, its white buildings clustered together in imitation of the larger cities of the West Indies. Patience took her into a pleasant, trendy boutique, demanding the owner, who turned out to be a great friend of Patience Frazer's. Between the two older women, Lexy was soon lost. She succumbed to a long sundress, with its shirred bodice and thin straps, in a shimmery batik. The rich coral color accented her deep tan, and gave added depth to her gray eyes, making her sun-streaked hair seem even lighter. The soft swirling skirt was odd against her bare legs after years of jeans. Lexy enjoyed the sensuous movement and feel as she paraded around the display room, her back straight, her head held high, a smile of delight on her face.

Persuaded to add a pair of high-heeled sandals to her purchases, she felt like a young girl again, anxious for her first party.

'It's been years since I've dressed like this,' she confessed as she circled the room once more, delaying her change back to jeans, reluctant to wait until evening to wear the pretty dress again.

'Why?' Patience boomed, tact gone by the wind.

'I found it gave men ideas. I've had trouble enough coping,' she replied. 'I'll change and be right out.'

She stopped long enough to purchase some coral lipstick and dark mascara, presenting her packages to be rung up. If either woman suspected the reason why she was indulging herself after so long, they refrained from commenting. Margaret Tremon, Patience's friend, was pleased Patience's guest found so much pleasure from the few things she was buying.

Patience kept a running monologue on the way home about Santa Theresa and her home there, her friends and neighbors. She had been in residence for over twelve years, being a retired schoolteacher. Lexy wondered faintly how her pupils had fared. Patience had probably forced them to learn, her loud voicing giving no excuse for not hearing the lessons.

Lexy learned that cotton was the important island crop and that one or two important families owned and worked most of the usable land. They would be coming to Land's End that evening, as well as the new doctor, the Mayor and his wife, Margaret and her husband, and one or two other friends of Dominic's.

'Dominic stays here a lot, you know. A boat's a fine enough house, but a body gets tired of rocking all the time. Robin always came before, don't reckon I'll see as much of him now.'

'Isn't there an air service here? I mean, Robin and Sarah could fly in and visit every so often, or you to Bridgetown.'

'Lord love you gal, this is a small island, two thousand people, give or take a few. No call for a regular air service. Charter plane, maybe. We're self-sufficient in most ways, but a tourist place we're not. No, our only inter-island service is the supply ship.'

'How often does one of those come?'

'Oh, I don't know, every week or so. Less frequently when hurricanes are springing up.'

Wondering how to pinpoint the next arrival time, Lexy asked how the cotton left the island.

'For that the owners charter special vessels. But that's later in the year, wouldn't bring Robin and Sarah here anyway. Here we are now. Don't show Dominic that dress, mind, we want to have him surprised.' Patience let out a hearty laugh as she drew up before her villa.

Exasperated at being so close to finding out the supply ship's schedule, but not getting the precise information she needed, Lexy got out of the car, dragging her bundles across the seat and carrying them to the house while Patience continued the car around to the garage. Lexy's thoughts were whirling. Maybe tonight she could ask one or two of the guests, they would think her only curious about island routine, thirsting for knowledge. She would have to try anyway. What if the ship came tomorrow? She wanted to be ready to leave on it when it was next due in.

So engrossed was she in trying to work out how she would ask her questions that evening that she almost bumped into Dominic in the dim light of the entry way.

'Shopping, I see,' he said eying her packages.

'Yes, I did get one or two things.' She moved past him, starting up the stairs.

'I would have picked up something for you when I was in town,' he said watching her.

'It's okay, Patience took me. She, uh, wanted to go in herself.'

'You're a shocking liar, Lexy,' he returned coolly. 'Coming to dinner tonight?'

'Yes.' She was almost at the top when she remembered. Turning, she asked, 'about the computer, can your friend fix it? Or at least recover the data?'

'He was able to save the hard drive. I ordered a new laptop. It will take a while.' Dominic shrugged.

'Oh.' Lexy could hardly keep the jubilation from her voice. She'd have time to plan her escape. 'See you later.'

She reached the top of the stairs and started down the hallway just as Patience entered the house. She could hear her voice carrying, the words stopping Lexy in her tracks.

'Hi Dominic, how was your day?'

'Fine, Aunt Patience. By the way, you needn't worry about those sleeping pills any more, I threw them away.'

'Did she tell you why she was taking them? She isn't sick, is she?' Patience's voice wafted upstairs. 'I was so surprised last night, when I went in to tell her to open her window as I shut off the air-conditioner each night, to see the bottle spilled out beside her. Honestly, you younger people!'

'I was furious when I found out. But she won't use them again. Come on and let's get a cold drink. Tell me, are the Hanson's coming tonight?'

Their voices faded as they left the entryway and Lexy slowly continued to her room. That at least explained how Dominic knew she had the pills. She bit her lip, remembering his anger and his hard fingers on her shoulders. She shook her head and went into her room forgetting the problems of the morning as she unfolded her new dress and lovingly put it on the hanger.

9

Lexy was almost sick with trepidation by the time she was ready to descend for the party. She hadn't been to a party in years. She was feeling shy and vulnerable and afraid of saying all the wrong things. She'd already heard two cars pull up, but couldn't force herself downstairs.

Again, she peeked into the mirror, still surprised at what she saw, a slender sophisticated woman; cheeks rosy with excitement, her lashes darkened, giving a lovely sooty appearance to her eyes, highlighting them, making them more mysterious than normal. The extra height form the heels gave her some confidence, the unaccustomed dress giving her courage. What would Dominic's reaction be? If she were honest with herself, she would like to knock him back on his heels. She smiled wryly at that notion. If anything, he'd suspect dressing this way as one of her wiles to entice him. Still, if he would only forget for one night and treat her courteously and kindly, she'd have a night to remember.

Lexy drew a deep breath. If she didn't go soon, everyone would have arrived and she would be making a grand entrance, and her stomach flipped over with that thought. With one more look in the mirror for courage, she was all set, when a knock at the door startled her, and she crossed the room to open it. 'Oh.'

Dominic stood before her, his dark hair brushed smooth, his blue eyes widening, then narrowing at the sight of her. He was wearing dark trousers and a light polo-necked shirt, displaying the strength of his shoulders, accentuating his height. His eyes went over her, noticing everything about her, the soft swell of her breasts, rising and falling in rapid motion; her slender waist; the soft feminine folds of her long skirt.

'Well, well, well. Lexy in a dress. You should do it more often, my sweet.'

'I'm glad you think so,' she murmured, her color high.

'Is this in my honor? Or for Aunt Patience?' he asked sardonically.

'Neither.' Lexy retorted recklessly, tired of his incessant needling, tired of always taking his verbal abuse. 'I understand there will be some eligible men here tonight. A girl needs to look to her future after all,' she said provocatively. Maybe she should fight fire with fire. If he thought she was one kind of woman, so be it.

His face hardened. 'Have you given me up as a choice, then, Lexy love?'

'I'm not one to beat a dead horse,' she said lightly, her heart thudding against the chill in his voice, the bleak look in his eyes. 'Cut my losses and move on, that's my motto. You're very forthright in your thoughts about me.' She shrugged.

'If I can put in a word for you, experience and all,' he drawled.

'No thanks. I'll manage.' She met his look, her chin tilted, her eyes defiant, but the bravado was fleeting as, she looked away first, apprehension returning. 'I guess we should go down,' she said reluctantly.

'Not cold feet, my dear? That will never do. Come, I want to watch a person of your caliber in action; I missed all the preliminary routine because of Joey's short cut to the truth. It should prove most interesting, most instructive.'

Her heart felt the jab, but she kept her composure. She would like to ruffle him once or twice, see his composure slip. She sighed, not a hope of penetrating his shell.

As Dominic turned, she preceded him down the hall to the stairs, faltering at the sight and sound of Patience's guests. More were joining the early arrivals, greetings being exchanged, drinks served.

Dominic's hand at her waist propelled her down the stairs—there was no turning back now. It was easier after the first introduction. Patience was her friend and introduced her as such to her neighbors. They were kind and courteous, welcoming Lexy to Santa Theresa. First Paul Martin, gray-haired, stately, the new doctor.

'New as you can see, only to Santa Theresa. I'm semi-retired, and this is an ideal place. Healthy lot, the people here.'

She greeted Margaret Tremon like an old friend, liking her stout husband, Victor, on sight. She was introduced to the mayor and his wife. Soon she met Susan Hartford, the retired schoolteacher, and young Elaine Hartford, Susan's granddaughter, who already knew Dominic.

'It seems odd to see you and not Robin with you, Dom, we'll have to have a quiet chat later and you can tell me how he and Sarah are getting along,' Elaine said.

'I'd like that,' he replied.

'Lexy.' Patience was at her elbow again, with two tall stocky men, Robert Preston and his son Evan. She made the introductions, and added, 'The Preston's are our biggest cotton growers here on Santa Theresa.'

'Welcome to Santa Theresa, visiting long?' Evan was immediately captivated by Lexy's sweet smile and sparkling gray eyes.

'No,' Dominic turned from speaking to Elaine and held out his hand to grip Evan's.

'Dominic! Didn't see you when we got here. How are you? Good to see you again. How's Robin? Seems funny not to have him along, too.'

'I know. He's doing fine. Hello, Bob.'

'Dominic. Good to see you. Miss Kent is a guest of your aunt's, too, I understand.'

'Actually Lexy came with me.'

Both Preston men's smiles froze, and they stared, first at Dominic, then at Lexy. Robert Preston remembered his manners first and looked away, but remained thoughtful. Evan was more vocal.

'Came with you? Lucky dog,' he smiled at Dominic, his maneuver returning quickly to Lexy.

'I crew for Dominic on the Marybeth.' Lexy was going to clear up the situation, then try to evade Dominic's presence. She didn't want a repetition of his comment aboard Bob Driscoll's yacht, not here, not tonight.

'You working on another book, Dominic?' Bob Preston asked. Evan, seeing his chance, deftly cut Lexy away from them and walked her towards the makeshift bar at the end of the room.

'Good old Dad, he can talk to Dom and I'll talk to you.'

Lexy smiled at his adroit maneuver. How nice he wanted to escape Dominic's presence. She asked Evan exactly what he did for a living, and he launched into a greatly exaggerated tale of cotton growing. Soon Lexy was laughing merrily, happy for the first time in many weeks. He introduced her to various other people, in passing, only letting her chat for a few minutes with each before whisking her away. Finally he drew her aside, scanning the gathering.

'There, I think that's all. Now you have met every body, Patience will be satisfied and you can devote the rest of the evening to me.'

'That sounds like fun, but shouldn't I mingle more?' She was flattered he went to so much trouble to have a little time alone with her. What a wonderful change from Dominic's condemnation.

'No, the party is for Dominic, too, let him do the mingling. I say, you did say you only crew for Dom, right?'

'Yes. He hired me for this journey because Robin's not available anymore.'

'Fine. I only ask because he hasn't taken his eyes off us all evening and it's decidedly unnerving. Don't want to poach on another man's preserves.'

She looked over her shoulder; her eyes meeting the dark blue brooding ones across the crowded room. Even in the midst of a group including Robert Preston and Elaine he was watching her. She glazed her eyes and passed him by, turning back to Evan with a wide smile, moving deliberately closer to him.

'Don't worry, he probably feels some sort of guardianship for me.' She tucked her arm in his. 'Do you think we could go and eat? I've seen several people with plates, and I'll admit to being a little peckish.'

'Thy wish is my command.' He bowed deftly, covering her hand with his and leading her to the buffet.

They loaded their plates from the vast assortment Molly had spent all day preparing and found a secluded table set at the edge of the veranda. The hum of voices was a soft background murmur, the air was still but cooler, the night sky was sparkling with stars. Evan asked Lexy about her sailing experience and the talk moved naturally to skin-diving. Upon discovering Lexy had diving experience, he became enthusiastic.

'I say, Lexy, we could do a little diving around here. I have scuba gear and a nice cruiser. What do you say?'

'Oh, I'd like that. I haven't been in a couple of years, though

I've been doing quite a bit of snorkeling in the lagoon where Dominic anchors.'

'How is that place?'

'It's lovely, peaceful, and so picturesque-pretty you almost think it's artificial.'

'Robin used to dive a little, he said he'd like scuba gear in the lagoon.'

'I've often thought that myself. I can only dive about ten feet at the most with the snorkel.' She sighed faintly. 'It was lovely, though.'

'I'll tell you what. I'll follow you up, bring my gear and we can dive while old Dominic writes. How about it?'

'Well,' Lexy hedged, if all went well, she would be gone from Santa Theresa before Dominic headed for the island again.

She slid a glance at Evan. He could tell her the schedule of the supply boat. He would surely know. If it visited the island once a week, it might be expected any time, even tomorrow. But she couldn't risk telling him why she wanted the information.

'That's a good idea,' she replied to his suggestion, her thoughts on how to find out the schedule.

'Good, that's settled then. I'll get the coordinates from Dom and follow after I stock up my boat. We'll be all set.'

She smiled faintly—wouldn't Dominic love that, if she were still going with him. She leaned closer to Evan, smiling into his eyes.

'Tell me about living here on Santa Theresa,' she invited.

'Yes, Evan, tell the little lady all about life on a cotton island.' Dominic hooked a foot over a nearby chair and drew it over. 'You don't mind if I join you?' He smiled sardonically at Lexy, pulling his chair near hers, sitting back, watchful and alert. 'Do go on.'

She bit her lip in consternation, glaring at him beneath her lashes. Darn, he would appear just when she had a chance to find something out naturally, without causing any comment. Now she would have to hope Evan would mention the steamer of his own accord, she wouldn't be able to question the schedule lest it alert Dominic to her plan. He was too astute not to suspect something was up. A small dart of disappointment and regret pierced her. If she succeeded in her plan she would never see the quiet island again, never swim in the silken waters of the lagoon, never walk along the white beach, follow the trail crisscrossing the island. Well, she would always have the memories, they would have to suffice. Memories of a paradise island and the man who could have made it heaven.

Evan saw nothing amiss with his friend's joining them and plunged into his stories of Santa Theresa. Lexy tried to forget Dominic's presence, laughed in all the right places, but her mind wasn't fully on Evan. She was too aware of Dominic, only inches away from her. Too afraid of what he might say or do. She flicked him a glance. He was watching her with that brooding concentration she was so familiar with. Why wouldn't he leave her alone? She had done him no harm.

At a pause in Evan's recital, Dominic looked with feigned surprise at Lexy's glass. 'Why, Lexy, your drink's gone.'

'Oh, I say, I didn't realize. I'll get you another.' Evan, eager to please, took her glass and disappeared towards the house.

'You did that deliberately,' she complained, turning to face him. 'Why can't you go mingle with the other guests. Leave me alone!'

'Now, Lexy, you know I'm trying to watch you in action, to get an idea of how femme fatales operate. While I don't need it for this book, I might sometime want a cheap little cheat work on the hero, what better opportunity to see firsthand how one does it? It'll make good copy.'

'No.'

'Now don't blow your act. I know continence is wearing, but you...' His taunting glib look was too much.

Crack! The sharp sound of the slap echoed around the terrace causing several heads to turn in their direction. Dominic reached out and yanked Lexy back to her chair, his hand tight at her wrist, the fingers biting into her flesh. She stared at the reddening mark on his face with horrified eyes. Trembling, she tried to speak.

'I'm sorry.' It came out a whisper.

She was appalled with her reaction to his words. What was happening to her? She'd tried so hard for years to remain cool, poised, in control. She had made a kind of life for herself, but lately she was losing that control. Why was Dominic so provoking? Why did he anger her so?

In the past, when men had made disparaging remarks, either in her hearing or to her face, she ignored them with an icy disdain, cloaking the hurt she felt, maintaining her composure and serenity to all outward appearances. She had worked hard through the years to develop the technique to ignore such insults, found it effective and easy to assume. Why with Dominic did she lose control, let him under her guard, let him know he hurt, he hit home?

He said not a word; his painful fingers transmitting his anger. Fearfully, Lexy glanced around the terrace. The guests had resumed their pursuits, no one was paying them any marked attention. They were alone. Alone at the edge of the dark velvet night. She was trembling slightly, stunned by her own savage behavior. Shocked that she had actually slapped Dominic in the face. Her eyes were drawn again to the red cheek; it must sting, be warm now. She ached to touch it lightly with her fingertips, her lips, to erase the memory of her hand. She swallowed hard, her eyes on Dominic.

'Don't ever do such a thing again,' he gritted. 'Thank your lucky stars Aunt Patience has a houseful of neighbors, or I would retaliate!'

'I am sorry, I shouldn't have done it. It was unforgivable,' she said, her voice low, sincere. Then, unable to stop she blurted out, 'But you caused it yourself. Stop antagonizing me. Stop calling me names and insulting me all the time. You know what I'm supposed to have done, if you don't like thinking of it when you look at me, stay away. Why do you throw it in my face all the time? What do you get out of denouncing me to everyone we meet? Even chance strangers like the Driscoll's and Martin's?'

'I don't know if you are proud of what you are, of what power you can wield over besotted men; or ashamed of the way you live. Why don't you stop it, if you are ashamed?

It's not a pretty way to live, it makes me sick,' he replied, his hand still a vice grip.

'When I want your opinion, I'll ask for it. May I have my wrist back, Evan is returning.'

Dominic threw her arm away and rose, just as Evan joined them.

'Excuse me, I'll see to our other guests.' He walked away, one cheek still decidedly redder than the other.

Evan watched him, almost forgetting Lexy's drink.

'Oh, I say, here's your drink. Was Dom mad?'

'No. Tell me more about the way you live here. I've never lived on so small an island. How do you get your groceries and all? Surely not everything is grown on the island.'

'We are on a regular routine shipping schedule. There's a company in Granada that distributes and transports cargo from the larger ports to the smaller islands like ours. We get a delivery once a week in good weather, every Thursday.' He sat down, still looking after Dominic with a puzzled look on his pleasant face.

Thursday—and tonight was Tuesday. Lexy sat back triumphant. Tomorrow she would see to gathering her things. Then Thursday somehow get to the town pier and beg or buy passage on the ship. She'd have all day tomorrow to think of a scheme to avoid Dominic and get to town with bag and baggage on Thursday. She'd plan it all out tomorrow, when she was alone and could think uninterrupted.

She felt a small quake of conscience at leaving Dominic deserted without a crewman. He had come to her aid in Santa Inez when she had needed work and had offered her the job. And, while she had promised before landing in Bridgetown to work the voyage for him, that was before Joey Compton's damaging revelations. Circumstances had changed. Maybe there would be someone here on the island who could do the job, even Evan or that girl Elaine. She looked happy enough to see Dom. Or, for that matter, Lexy was sure Patience would be delighted to have Dominic stay here with her while he wrote. There was nothing that said he had to write on a boat.

The party began breaking up. Gradually, sporadically, the people were leaving. Patience sought Lexy and had her standing by Dominic to help bid their guests goodnight. Evan was one of the last to leave, and he pulled Lexy a little aside from the others while his father was making his farewells, to tell her he would stop by the next afternoon to see if she would be free to dive. She agreed and they parted amiably.

'Thank you, Aunt Patience, it was a nice gathering,' Dominic said as the last guests drove off, their taillights dwindling down the drive.

'I had a nice evening, too, Patience. Thank you. And thanks too for urging me to get the dress,' Lexy murmured, glad it was all over. She pulled the skirt out, letting it fall. She wished briefly that they'd had dancing; it would be a nice dress to dance in.

Involuntarily, she remembered the last time she had been dancing, on Driscoll's yacht, and her eyes flew to Dominic. He was studying his shoes, however, and not looking at her.

'I'm glad you both enjoyed yourselves. It is a nice group, don't you think? I'm lucky to have nice friends.' She switched off lights as she talked. 'Well, off to bed now. I'm tired, I don't mind saying. Molly will cope with this mess in the morning. Go on up, go on up.' She shooed them before her like children.

'Goodnight,' Lexy called as she slipped into her room.

Despite the late hour, she was a long time falling asleep, her body craving the artificial inducement it was used to. She relived the party, especially her shameful behavior with Dominic. She winced again remembering the sound of her hand on his face, his eyes flashing surprise and pain before he clamped down and veiled them. She recalled, too, his words.

She was ashamed of what she had done, so many years ago now, but recent events were a direct result of ugly gossip and jealous backbiting. What was she to do to expiate her sins? She was circumspect in her life, avoiding anything that would substantiate any part of the accusations about her, trying to avoid being put in similar circumstances again. Though, she supposed, crewing for Dominic could be misconstrued by some. Restlessly she tossed and turned on her bed, finally dropping off to an uneasy sleep.

'Come on, Lexy, let's get going!' Dominic was pounding on her door. 'Hurry up.'

'What do you want?' she called out sleepily, opening one eye. It was still gray outside, just dawn. 'Ohhh,' she rolled over and buried her head in her pillows. 'Go 'way,' she moaned. It was much too early to get up. It had been late when they'd retired, even later before she finally slept, and she certainly didn't want to get up early after all that, just to sight see around Santa

Theresa, or visit, or whatever else Dominic had in mind.

'Come on, girl, I'm ready to go. You're holding me up.' He smacked his hand hard against her door.

'Dominic, what's going on?' Patience's voice boomed from across the hall.

Lexy found herself growing awake with the effort to hear his reply. The door muffled his words, but they satisfied Patience, because Lexy heard her door close. Ah, silence again. Her eyes closed.

The sudden click of her door opened them again. Dominic was standing in the frame, fully dressed in jeans and a cotton pullover. His hair still damp from his shower. 'Listen, Lexy, I can't keep yelling, it's annoying Aunt Patience. Get dressed and move it. I'm ready to sail and if you are not downstairs in ten minutes, I'll carry you to the boat as you are.'

He closed the door before Lexy could gather her wits, before she realized he meant to leave Santa Theresa today, right now. Before she could tell him she wasn't going with him.

She sat up, her thoughts in turmoil. Why was he leaving now? What about his computer? What about her chance for the island supply ship? She scrambled into a top and jeans. She would go down and tell him he would have to get somebody else. She pulled on her shoes. He wouldn't welcome the news. In fact he'd probably be quite angry, but she'd stand firm. She didn't understand, though, because the computer couldn't be ready yet.

He stood in the front doorway watching the sea when she appeared at the head of the stairs, turning when he heard her descending. He frowned, noting her appearance, minus her bag.

'Get your things,' he reminded her impatiently.

'I'm not going,' she faltered, stopping halfway down.

'Not going?' he repeated perplexed. 'Not going where? I'm ready to sail.'

'You'll have to get somebody else to crew,' she said, holding on to the railing tightly. 'I'm quitting. I'll catch a lift on the island supply ship when it calls and be out of your life.'

'What the bloody hell are you talking about?' He crossed to the bottom step, glaring up at her, his hands on his hips, anger evident in his very stance, his look stony. 'You signed on for the whole trip, sweetheart, until the book is finished. This side-trip was unplanned, but doesn't alter our arrangement. Just because you've met a rich planter and find it more lucrative to chat him up, doesn't mean you're leaving me hanging!'

Lexy sank slowly down on the step, her legs too weak to hold her. Did Dominic really think she was leaving him to try and captivate Evan Preston? He couldn't be serious, she had only been joking last night.

'That's not the reason and you know it,' she protested vainly. 'I just can't take any more of your snide comments, your . . . taunting me and . . .' she trailed off, miserably aware of his scornful look, his rigid stance. She licked her lips. What was the use to try to explain?

'I don't blame her!' Patience's voice surprised them. Neither had noticed her appearance at the top of the stairs. Her iron-gray hair flying every which way, her bathrobe pulled hastily over her gown, she frowned down at them. 'I think if you apologize for your sometimes hasty tongue, my boy, she'll go gladly. Do so, and get going. I need my rest and can't get it with you two shouting all over my house.' She stood solidly by, fixing her nephew with a compelling eye.

Dominic stared at his aunt, then dropping his eyes to the woman crumpled on the steps. 'I beg your pardon for any unwarranted insults or hasty words I have said to you,' he said with exaggerated politeness.

Lexy's head jerked with his emphasis on unwarranted, but

before she could speak, Patience again broke in.

'Good, good. Now get your things, Lexy. You can't ask better than that. Hurry up, girl. Dom's in a hurry and I'm tired.'

Lexy turned and slowly climbed the stairs, her shoulders drooping, her head lowered. Patience would never ally herself against her nephew, never countenance helping Lexy leave Dominic while he still had need of her help. Slowly she made her way to her room. The older woman watched her go past, remaining at the top of the stairs to bid her farewell.

Lexy gathered her clothes, folding them and stuffing them into her large denim shoulder bag. She opened the closet and took a long look at her pretty coral dress, letting the soft folds of material cascade through her fingers.

Briefly she remembered some of the magic she had felt when she had first put it on. But she would have no need of it in the future. She sighed, it had been fun to dress up again, primp and be feminine. Slowly she closed the door. Perhaps Patience would know somebody who could use it.

Patience was still waiting at the top of the stairs, of Dominic there was no sign. Lexy smiled tremulously at her hostess.

'Thank you for a nice visit, Patience. I didn't know we were supposed to leave so soon. Evan is coming by today, we were to go diving. Would you explain for me, apologize?'

'Sure, child.' Patience was worried. 'I hope I've done right. I think I have.' Her voice was low and troubled. 'You do love my nephew, don't you, Lexy?'

Lexy looked towards the door where Dominic had been standing; the tall, unyielding man she had known for such a short time. His dark hair so often tousled from the wind or from running his fingers through it when he worked; the blue eyes, so cold and condemning, yet able to be warm and appealing on occasions; his brown body, strong and dependable; his kindness when she was sick; the humor they had shared in Bridgetown; his rigid ideals and principles; his way with words, all going together to make him the complex individual he was. A clever man, writer of more than a dozen books, giving reading pleasure to millions. A quixotic, chivalrous man, faithful to his dead wife whom his aunt thought not good enough for him. She sighed gently and turned back.

'Yes, I love him so much I ache with it,' she confessed. 'But I think he hates me,' she whispered, pain and distress reflected in her eyes. She tried a smile, giving Patience a quick hug.

'Goodbye, I'm glad I met you.'

She hurried down the stairs, Patience's hearty goodbye ringing in her ears. As she went out the door to the first rays of the sun, she saw Dominic pacing impatiently on the terrace. Well, she was committed, she wouldn't be leaving on the island ship, but going back to the isolated world she loved and hated. To be with him was a joy, when he offered friendship, a truce. His hard-cutting accusations a pain only to be borne. Would she ever escape from it?

'I'm ready,' she called.

As they walked quickly to the pier, Lexy skipping every so often to keep pace with his long stride, she paused once—was she really going with him? She could still pull back, though he would probably toss her over his shoulder and take her on board. She resumed walking. She hated scenes, and it wasn't fair on Patience. But the real reason she was on the pier walking towards the Marybeth was simple; she would rather be with him and have an occasional truce then never see him again. All too soon the day would come when he finished the book, the cruise would end, and she would be gone from his life. It was not in her to hasten that day now. She would try it a little longer.

She asked him about his computer.

'I've taken Simon's. He'll get the new one when it's delivered. He got the data from the hard drive and loaded it on his machine. I'm right where I should be and am anxious to get back to work. Once the sails are set and we're on course, I'll get to it right away. I hate the delay when I'm in the mood.'

'We should have put on water . . .' she trailed off as he helped her on board, his hands sending waves of awareness up her arms.

'Water, gas, fruits, restocked can goods, all taken care of yesterday. What did you think I did all day while you and Aunt Patience were out buying up Santa Theresa?'

She made no comment. She'd have several hours respite before having to face him once he began work, and her spirits rose a little. They were aboard the Marybeth and she loved sailing—life wasn't all bad.

They reached the island long before sunset, having had a good steady wind off the starboard quarter all the way. Lexy's face broke into a delighted smile when she sighted it on the horizon. She was surprised at the strong feeling of homecoming that washed over her. Tomorrow, she would swim and dive, maybe fetch the dinghy and go to the fresh-water pool. It was good to be back.

10

The next few days passed idyllically for Lexy. She rediscovered the pleasures of the lagoon, and she found the somewhat battered dinghy high on the beach where Dominic had dragged it after the storm. Dragging it back to the water's edge was no easy task, but Dominic was already at work and Lexy wanted no delay. It floated, but look as she might, only one small part of an oar came to light. So she swam back to the sloop. In the back of her mind was the picture of another set of oars. She tried the outside lockers, but no luck.

Slowly she went below. If she fixed Dominic's lunch, when he ate it, she could ask him about the extra oars. He was oblivious to her presence, his eyes fixed on the laptop's screen, the words pouring across. Even when Lexy placed the lunch before him, he did not notice.

'Lunch, Dominic,' she said firmly.

'Huh?' He stopped typing with a frown. 'What?'

'Lunch.' She pointed to his plate on the table.

He stretched his arms out, rotating his shoulders to loosen the tension. Unexpectedly he smiled at her. 'Shall we eat it topside? It's warm down here.'

Surprised, she concurred, warily wondering what he was up to.

To Lexy's continued surprise, he was pleasant throughout the entire break.

'How did you spend your morning?' he inquired when they were settled by the helm, their feet almost touching in the well.

'I swam to the beach, got the dinghy re-floated, but can't find the oars.' She was having a difficult time keeping her eyes off him, so great was the change. He was almost the man she had known in Bridgetown, had liked so much. How long would this last?

'Spare oars are with the foul-weather gear,' he offered casually. 'Go inland at all?'

'No, thought I might later.'

'Umm. If you go after three or so, I'll come too,' he said, studying the island, seeing little change evident from the lagoon save the vegetation debris scattered along the once pristine beach.

Lexy swallowed her amazement and gave a small noncommittal reply. She really didn't know what to make of this change.

She swam later in the afternoon, and went with Dominic to see what damage had been done from the recent storm. They explored on a friendly footing, both pleased so little had changed. There were dead palm fronds and bits of debris along some of the pathways, but most of the tropical vegetation had escaped any real damage.

Lexy gave up trying to understand Dominic's behavior, glad he was calling a halt to hostilities, pleased he would spend some time with her.

As the days slowly passed, they continued in their new-found peace. While Dominic worked as if driven many hours each day to make up for the time lost, he would deliberately take time out to dine with Lexy, swim with her occasionally, or row to the island and aimlessly walk around, following the faint paths and trails together. Their talk was stilted at first, as topics were gingerly offered, slowly explored. Dominic spoke of his life in the West Indies, his childhood, escapades he and Robin had been involved in over the last twenty years. He and Lexy discussed books, plays, ideal cars, or a fantasy vacation—Lexy's at the Ritz in Paris, Dominic's skiing in

the Alps. Once or twice Lexy inadvertently let slip something of her life with Miles Jackson, or her early years in England. Dominic would grow distant then, cutting short whatever activity they were engaged in, curt and formal until the next time.

Lexy remembered the fun she'd had with him in Bridgetown when they'd seen Sam Lord's Castle, their shared laughter, their close ideas in so many things. Some of that closeness found them here on the island. They would laugh again and be carefree for a time.

Lexy began to hope, to grow optimistic for the first time in a long while. She knew they were growing closer, an understanding seemed to be springing up between them. For herself she would guard it well. She loved him so and cherished each moment spent with him. There would be no Joey Compton to shatter it this time.

One afternoon, while Dominic was working, Lexy took one of his earlier books to the pond and stayed all afternoon to reread it, the dappled shade of the trees sheltering her from the fierce sun. It was a good, well-written story. She recognized his style and one or two phrases that he had carried over to his current effort.

She lay back and wondered how much longer it would take him to finish this book. With all supplies replenished, they could stay here at the island another four weeks or so before restocking. He'd be close to finishing the draft in another week if he kept up this rate. She remembered what he'd said, that was the worst part of a book, writing the first draft. Then he had to polish it, refine it, tighten it up; and run through it again for continuity. Then it would be ready for his publishers.

She watched the palm fronds move slowly against the blue sky, their spikes overlapping as each higher frond cut more light. In all likelihood, they would have to replenish supplies once more before he was finished. Then what? Would he say anything? Ask her to stay, or was this pleasant interlude just his way of making it easier all round to work in peace and harmony. Would he be glad when the book was finished and he didn't require Lexy Kent's crewing services any longer? Was he just biding his time until then?

Sighing, she renewed her plans for immigrating to Canada. She really liked the West Indian climate, who wouldn't, but it would be so much harder to stay now, always living with the chance she would run into Dominic, the hope she would. Closing her eyes, she tried to relax, giving up temporarily all thoughts and worries of the future—time enough for that later. She dozed off.

When she awoke, slowly and peacefully, she glanced around. The sun was gone from behind the palm trees, shining now lower in the western sky. It was far longer than she had planned to be gone, but she obviously had needed the sleep. Since the loss of the sleeping pills, she had difficulty in falling asleep at night. She rubbed her eyes, then stretched, ending by sitting up. With a rueful laugh, she reflected she would probably have trouble sleeping this night as well.

Lexy was surprised to see another boat in the lagoon when she reached the white sandy beach. For a brief moment she thought that Bob Driscoll had returned, but quickly saw the boat was not Bob's large Chriscraft, but a smaller, dark blue cruiser, its stern turned away, its registration conveying nothing to her. She rowed the dinghy to the sloop, making it fast and clambering aboard. She could hear the low murmur of voices in the cabin. As she went down the steep stairs she experienced a strong feeling of deja vu. Dominic was sitting on one bench of the table, facing her, like he had been that fateful morning in Bridgetown. Across from him a man with brown hair sat, talking, now turning to see the newcomer.

'Whew,' Lexy let out a sigh of relief. 'Hello Evan, I didn't expect you.' She smiled and dropped her book on the counter. She had stood just here that morning. But Evan was no Joey. She had no reason to fear his visit.

'He said you did expect him,' Dominic said evenly. 'Said you discussed his coming here so you two could do some diving.'

Evan smiled at her, certain of his welcome. 'Here I am. Sorry I missed you the other day.'

'I am too; I didn't realize we were leaving Santa Theresa so soon. But I am surprised to see you.' She shot a quick glance to Dominic. 'I know we talked about it, but nothing definite was set. I thought you needed to find the co-ordinates from Dominic.'

'Patience knew them.' Evan said cheerily. 'I filled my tanks and here I am. I say, it is all right, Dom?' A shadow of doubt crept in.

'Sure, just don't expect me to join in. I'm busy.' Dominic's voice was cold; his eyes already back on his computer.

Lexy took his hint. 'Come out on deck with me, Evan, he's busy.' She grabbed three drinks from the cooler, opening them and putting one beside Dominic. Taking the others she led the way topside, going towards the bow, sitting on the deck and leaning against the cabin wall. She motioned with her hand for

Evan to sit beside her, and offered him a bottle.

'No problem in my coming, is there?' he asked uncertainly.

'No,' she said calmly, gazing off to the beach. Would it be a problem? Would he cause a change again?

'Dominic works hours every day on his book, really works. One of the requirements for my job was to leave him alone to get on with it. He. . . oh, I guess he loses his train of thought if interrupted and then gets annoyed. Actually he'll probably thank you for swimming with me, save him more aggravation.'

Evan relaxed with that. 'Why's that?'

Lexy explained their arrangement for swimming, and then changed the subject to find out more about the diving gear Evan had brought. It was too late to dive that day, but they made plans to try it first thing in the morning.

'I've got to fix supper now,' Lexy said, draining her bottle. 'I don't know what Dominic will want to do about it. You're welcome to eat with us, but a lot of days Dominic doesn't stop to eat, just eats as he works and I eat up here.'

'Come over and eat on my boat,' Evan offered.

Shaking her head slowly, she declined. It might be fun, but would surely give Dominic reason to think she was slacking on her job, and she would be seeing enough of Evan.

And so it proved over the next few days. Lexy enjoyed Evan's company. They used his diving tanks, exploring the entire lagoon, recharging the tanks when they got low with the compressor he brought which ran on a generator. She showed him over the island, rediscovering parts of it she had seen with Dominic, pleased Evan found it as enchanting as she did. They swam and sunbathed together, talked and laughed. Gone was the friendly time with Dominic, however. He was working now, hours every day and into the night on two occasions. Lexy regretted their lost closeness, regretted Evan's coming, but there was nothing she could do about any of it now, just play the cards fate kept dealing her.

Evan and Lexy spent every morning together, but she always returned to the sloop in time to fix Dominic's lunch, resting in the afternoon as Evan did during the heat of the day, only to meet again for more swimming. She ate on his boat one night, preparing Dominic's meal first as he declined the invitation in order to work.

The holiday atmosphere continued until, inevitably, one morning on the beach, Evan kissed her. They had been exploring over the island, clad in jeans and pullover shirts to protect them from the branches and bushes. Collecting some of the many flowers growing wild around the island, they gaily made their way back to the beach, promptly festooning the dinghy with the colorful blooms. In the exuberance of the moment, Evan caught her close and kissed her.

Lexy smiled slightly at his kiss, but her eyes were wary.

'Just for friendship's sake, and because I'm in such a good mood,' he explained. 'Row me back to my boat and I'll take your picture in this bower of flowers.'

She relaxed. 'All right. Then I'll fix Dom's lunch and rest. Are we diving later?'

'I say, most assuredly.'

Lexy dropped Evan at his boat, posed for the picture, then with a saucy grin, rowed for the sloop. Her heart skipped a beat when she saw Dominic's dark visage watching her from the deck of the Marybeth. She secured the dinghy and climbed reluctantly aboard.

'Your machinations seem well under way,' he said when she reached the deck.

'What do you mean?' Her heart sank. He was angry again.

'Your calculated plan to captivate a wealthy patron, what

else? What strong lures did you throw out for Evan to follow you here, after only one evening's acquaintance, and have him hang around for the best part of a week?'

'We are just friends, that's all. As to his staying, maybe he's taking a holiday.' She felt the old pain wash over her. It had meant nothing, all the happy hours when she thought that they might be drawing closer, reaching an understanding. It all had meant nothing to Dominic.

'Complete with shipboard romance. How far has it gone, when you and Evan go off into the island for hours at a time, how far do you go? Has he made love to you yet? Does he know how many men you have slept with before? Does he know what a little liar you are?' Dominic bit the words off, his voice cold and expressionless.

She shook her head against his questions, her distress growing. Why did he do this to her? 'Stop it, Dominic!'

'How far are you planning to go, hoping for marriage? Shall I tell the good Evan about you tonight, at dinner? Tell him about your past, about your indiscretions and . . .' his hoarse voice droned into her ear, the accusing words hammering at her brain. Her eyes filled with tears. She would not stand for this. She wouldn't let him keep on!

'Shut up, I don't want to hear. Shut up!' She put her hands over her ears, turning her back on him.

Ruthlessly he pulled her hands down, forcing her around, forcing her to listen. 'Why, Lexy, why? Why shouldn't Evan know what he's getting into? He's a nice enough guy. A word to the wise first won't hurt, just change the rules a little. I wouldn't want any friend of mine caught up by a cheap little tramp like you.'

'Who set you up as my judge, jury and executioner? You don't even know the facts,' she cried. 'What gives you the right to torment me? Leave me alone, Dominic. Leave me alone!'

'That I won't do,' he bit out, his hands tightening painfully on her wrists. 'I've paid your fine salary for very little service rendered. Surely Miles Jackson got more for his money. Four years, for God's sake!'

'Shut up, you're vile. Vile! You don't pay me enough for that,' she spat out, struggling to free herself. To her surprise, his hands released her, only to take her by the arm, dragging her towards the cabin.

A touch of fear coursed through her. 'Let me go, Dominic.'

'We'll up the stakes,' Dominic said savagely, thrusting her ahead of him.

'No, oh no,' she whispered, trying to hold back, trying to brace herself against his push, but to no avail. Steadily, inexorably, he forced her forward, till he picked her up and tossed her on her bunk.

She sat up, scrambling back against the bulkhead, eyes wide with fear, her heart beating rapidly, her mouth dry. Mesmerized, terrified, she watched him pull his shirt from his head, his hands go to his belt, then stop.

'Dominic! For God's sake, don't do this, please.' She was staring, unable to believe her own eyes. This couldn't be happening to her. It was surely a nightmare from which she would soon awake.

He reached for her.

The move galvanized her into action. Lexy fought, flailing her fists, trying to kick him, bite him, anything to escape. She was like a wild creature, cornered and fighting for survival. Raking her nails down his shoulder, she drew blood, but didn't stop him. Dominic lay across her, forcing her down, heavy on her, pinning her to the bunk, clawing at her top, seeking the soft skin beneath. Lexy twisted and turned, kicking out again and again, hitting him with her hands, trying desperately to evade him. Panting with exertion, her breath mingling with his as he sought supremacy, flesh smacking against flesh, she brought up her knee. Aiming for another target, she kneed him in his diaphragm as he moved to pull off her shirt. The short, unexpected jerk knocked the breath from Dominic. He lay still, winded.

Lexy quickly scrambled to the foot of her bunk, on her knees, facing him, her hands curled into claws, ready to defend again, her breath ragged and hoarse, terror still in her eyes.

Slowly Dominic drew breath again, once, twice. He slitted his eyes and saw her, his face distorting at her expression. Slowly he sat up, remaining on the edge of the bunk, his face buried in his hands.

The silence dragged on.

Lexy took a shaky breath. Watching him warily, she began to speak, softly, slowly.

'When I was seventeen, I thought I was in love with a man I knew from my hometown. We went everywhere together. Then, I had him to our house, but my grandfather, he raised me you know, forbade me to see him again, forbade me to have anything further to do with him. Grandfather said he was a rotter, only after my virtue to try to force my hand in marriage for grandfather's money,' she said flatly. 'I knew better, or so I thought. So, when I turned eighteen, I told him, my friend, I was of age and we could do whatever he wanted. Thumb our noses at my grandfather and his old cautions. I think I must have hurt my grandfather very much.' She looked closely at Dominic; he hadn't moved, was he listening to her? He owed her that much at least.

'Anyway, we went off for a weekend together. I left a note for my grandfather, made a grand gesture. And fell flat on my face. Before the weekend was over, his estranged wife showed up and made a horrible scene. I hadn't known he was married. And the worst part was he was after grandfather's money. I was just his ticket to an easier life.'

'You returned home sadder, but wiser.' He was listening.

'Yes. I tried to tell Grandfather that I realized my mistake. That I wanted his forgiveness. I would do anything to get back in his good graces.'

'You were young. He knew that.' Dominic said.

She laughed mirthlessly at that, a short bleak sound.

'Grandfather wouldn't believe me. He was furious. I was sent away, away from the only home I had ever had. It was horrible, Dominic, you can't imagine. I was young, had led a sheltered life and didn't know what to do. I had no money, no friends. It was awful.' Her eyes looked beyond him, back down the years to that young, bewildered and hurt teenaged girl. Alone for the very first time, frantic, unsure, afraid, prey to scandal, unhappiness, propositions and vicious gossip. She shrugged, sighed, coming back to the present.

'You know the rest. I hit up an old school friend for enough money to get to London. Got a job on a ship bound for the West Indies. Then met Miles. It was only, in spite of what that cat he married says. I was never his lover. Tom was his friend and he gave me a job when Amelia made it too uncomfortable to stay working with Miles. But by then Amelia, jealous as she was, spread lies all over Barbados. I had told Miles why I had left England and he had helped me when I first came over. She embellished it to fit her story, and told Joey, I guess.'

'Did he really ask you to live with him?' a tight voice, his head still in his hands.

'Yes, but he wasn't the only one. I couldn't make anyone believe I didn't want that, that I wasn't just playing hard to get. I was rather unkind when I refused your cousin. I know he relished our meeting in Bridgetown, he paid me back with interest.' Lexy shuddered at the remembrance—-Joey had been cruel. She glanced up to Dominic. Finally she had told him, now he would know.

'And Evan, what did you say to him to entice him this far from home? He's never taken his boat so far before. What promises did you offer him?' he bit out.

Lexy sighed, her fingers relaxing. She watched her hands, folding them loosely in her lap, her breathing back to normal. The danger was gone for now and oddly, she felt no further pain that Dominic didn't believe her, only a certainty that she must now go. Somehow, through all she'd suffered, the hope that she would find a way to tell him the truth, that he would love her and declare it as soon as she had told him the truth, had sustained her.

She never once envisioned his not believing her. She had only looked for a chance to explain.

She wasn't herself anymore, she was someone else, watching Alexis Kent to see what she would do now.

Dominic sat up, dropped his hands and slowly turned to face her. 'What about Evan?' he demanded harshly.

Still watching her hands, still with that detached feeling, Lexy replied softly,

'Please leave my cabin.' She said no more, her eyes closing wearily, shutting out all sights, just as she wished she could shut everything else out of her mind and forget.

She heard the click as the door closed.

11

Alexis turned the corner into the quiet street, squat palms lining both sides, giving large patches of shade in the late afternoon sun. The air was still and heavy, and she walked quickly the short distance to her apartment, her short skirt swinging with her firm step. She opened the outer door of the building, running lightly up the stairs to the second floor, almost blind in the faint light after the brilliance of the afternoon sun. Still, she knew her way by now and could have managed in the dark.

'Looking for you, Miss Kent,' a voice wheezed behind her.

Lexy turned to see her landlady trudging up the stairs, her huge girth almost too wide for the stairway.

'Is something wrong, Mrs. Taylor?' Lexy asked, puzzled. In the eight months she had lived here she had only seen Mrs. Taylor eight times—the first of each month, when paying her rent. With her vast bulk, Lexy could understand her landlady's reluctance to move about much. Yet, here she was, climbing the stairs, a small brown wrapped parcel in her hand.

'Whew! It's a hot day for these stairs,' Mrs. Taylor wheezed, reaching the top. 'Ain't nothing wrong. This parcel's for you. Gentleman brought it by today and asked me especially to deliver it to your hands.' Her brown eyes looked at Lexy slyly, 'He didn't give no name.'

Puzzled, Lexy thanked her and took the box. The brown

wrapper gave no clue as to its contents, or who had sent it. She took it and turned back to open her door. Her address was clearly printed, but that was all, no return address. No postage. She frowned. Only two or three people knew where she lived. Who could have brought it by?

Lexy, savoring the suspense, dropped it on the table in the main room as she crossed to switch on the fan. It was always warm in the afternoons here, stuffy. She was glad she worked in a shop with air-conditioning.

Fixing herself a tall glass of juice, with lots of ice, she kicked off her high-heeled sandals as she crossed the small room. She still preferred going barefoot. She smiled as she wiggled her toes, the pile of the small rug soft against her feet. Maybe one day Mr. Ferguson would let her work sans shoes.

Lexy crossed to the sofa, picking up the parcel in passing, sinking back into the soft cushions. She was pleasantly tired; an early night was on the cards this evening. She put her head back, sipped the juice, idly fingering the brown paper, relaxing from the day's activities.

Stacey, the accountant at Mr. Ferguson's bookshop where Lexy now worked, would be screaming with impatience to see what was inside the package, to discover who had sent it. Lexy smiled, maybe Stacey herself had sent it, she was one of the few people who knew her address. She could have had one of her friends bring it by. Mr. Ferguson also knew her address, but he wouldn't be sending her anything, nor would Stacey, come to that.

Lexy had been in Bridgetown for eight months. She remembered vaguely, finally, leaving the sloop after the awful realization and acceptance that her words had meant nothing to Dominic Frazer. She had not been believed. Dominic had been lying down in the main cabin, but asleep, or so she thought, though the air had reeked of brandy, when she sneaked out at dusk, with only her clothes, leaving everything else behind. Numbly, detached, she had sought Evan Preston's aid in surreptitiously leaving the lagoon; had obtained transportation at Santa Theresa, with no one knowing but Evan. How quick he'd been to come to her aid, but how puzzled.

Slipping away before dawn, sneaking into Santa Theresa, Lexy knew he had thought it highly dramatic, but she hadn't cared. She would forever be grateful for his help, but had been firm in bidding him farewell, with no forwarding address provided, although he had asked her more than once. She was cutting all ties.

Bridgetown was only to have been the departure point for another destination, but by the time she had reached the bustling anonymous city, the urgency to go so far had faded. By searching for a flat and a job in the older part of town, Lexy thought she would minimize any chance of running into former acquaintances. And so it had proved for the most part. Once she had run into Joey Compton who expressed his surprise at seeing her and quickly tried to engage her in a conversation. She had ended the encounter, vowing to avoid that street whenever possible thereafter. Another time she thought she had seen Amelia Jackson, and though Lexy did wonder how Miles was doing, she had no desire to renew acquaintances with his wife; so had turned and gone in another direction.

Her job at the bookshop had been most fortuitous. The proprietor's granddaughter wanted an extended leave to have a baby, and Lexy was glad of the opportunity to work, both because she needed the money, and because she needed the occupation to keep her thoughts at bay. While the job was not forever, the few months' respite would give her time to think and decide on her next move. Peggy was not sure if she wanted to leave little Jeffie, so the job could become permanent. It was now up to Lexy to decide to stay or try Canada.

She worked hard, but socialized very little outside of work. The few friends she'd made at the bookshop asked her to join them often, but she always refused. The hurt lurking in her eyes kept them from pressing the issue. They continued to ask her, accepting her refusals equably. She would come when she was ready.

She tried to banish all thoughts of Dominic from her mind, refusing to allow herself even a moment's memory before ruthlessly cutting it from her mind. This was easy enough to do during the day; she had plenty to do to occupy her mind. Still, in the nights, uncontrollable longings would sweep over her until she thought she would die with aching. She would then read until the small hours, trying to tire herself enough to sleep.

Eight months were not long enough to get over him, she thought, maybe eight years.

'Or eighty,' she said, draining her glass, wondering where he was now, what he was doing. Did he ever think of her?

Slowly Lexy unwrapped the parcel; staring in disbelief at the big letters on the book's cover. Jungle Gold by Nick Roberts. The colorful cover picture showing a sinister, dark mine swamped by jungle growth. Lexy sat frozen. It was his book. Dominic's book. It was published! Of course she knew from Mr. Ferguson's place that it was coming out, but they weren't expecting a shipment for another month or so. Time, she had thought, to be prepared, to be ready to deal with it.

Now, here was a copy in her lap. Tenderly her fingers traced the title, traced his pen name. This was the book he had written while she swam in the lagoon, explored the island, was sleeping in his bunk after being so sick. These words came from his head, through his fingers, now to her. She hadn't been there to see the finished manuscript, to read the ending. She would have to read the book. She smiled, remembering she had said that at Patience's.

Who had sent it?

She looked up, the color draining from her face. Oh, God, he couldn't know she was here. There was no way. She hadn't told anyone that knew him. Except for Joey, she had not run into any of Dominic's friends or relatives that she knew of. And Joey didn't know where she lived; their encounter had been on a public street near the shop. How did the book get here?

She shook the wrappings, but there was no card. Slowly she opened the book, there was nothing written on the inside cover. With a curious disappointment, she turned the page. The title jumped out at her again, then his name, his pen name. She smiled. She had liked what she had read before. She would read a little, just to see if she could spot where he had made changes from the first draft. Find out the ending.

A knock on the door delayed her plans. Her heart leaped. Could it be Dominic? Had he brought the book earlier and was now coming to– To what? Renew old acquaintances? Get angry at her leaving before the end of the writing? Lexy put the book down on the table and slowly crossed to open the door. Her mouth was dry, her heart pounding. Dominic?

Her heart dropped even as her defenses rose. It was not Dominic, but Joey Compton standing on the threshold.

'Hello, Lexy, remember me?' he asked insolently. His smile hinted at cruelty, his look raking her as she stood by the opened door.

'Go away, Joey,' she said as she started to close the door, but even as she began, he pushed it open, and walked into the flat.

'That's no way to treat an old friend, honey,' he said easily, smiling at her discomfort. While not a particularly tall man, Lexy felt as if he towered over her. Why was he here?

'We are not friends, please leave.' Lexy remained by the opened door, watching Joey with hostile eyes. He was the last person she had wanted to see.

'Thought we could visit a while, you know. Talk over old times, so to speak, maybe talk about our future. Left Dominic, eh—'

'I haven't seen your cousin in months. And thanks to you and your horrible revelations on the boat the job was awful. That was mean, Joey. It would have been a good job.'

He shrugged, looking around the small living room, his eye caught by the wrapping paper and the new book. He picked it up. 'Well, well, Dom's through another book and you already have a copy. Any good?'

He idly turned the first few pages, glancing at the title, stopping as something caught his eye.

'Put it down and get out!' Lexy said, wanting to snatch the precious book from his hands as if his very touch would defile it.

Joey looked at her curiously for a moment, closed the book and dropped it casually back on the table.

'Seen Dom lately?' he asked, with an odd note in his voice.

'No, I told you, it's been months since I've seen him. Will you get out!'

Lexy debated calling on her landlady for help in evicting Joey, but knew it would be futile. Even if Mrs. Taylor were willing to get involved, Joey would probably charm her out of the notion. He was a nice enough looking man and could play up to the ladies.

'Told you that day on the boat that he was still wrapped up in his dead wife—he's not for the likes of you, Lexy girl.'

'And I suppose you are?' she asked sarcastically. She sighed, moving slowly away from her stance at the door. If Joey came only to bait her, her best defense would be to ignore him. If he tired of the activity, maybe he'd leave.

'I'm still willing,' he glanced around again. 'I could move right in here, this is a nice place.' His smile was almost a leer.

'You're disgusting!' she replied. 'How did you find out where I live?' Gone now was her cloak of anonymity which she had tried to erect, her carefully built new life.

'Followed you back to your shop the day we ran into each other. Later, followed you here.' He shrugged and crossed to her. 'It was easy enough, and well worth it. Lexy, I still want you,' he said with urgency.

She stiffened and turned to face him. 'Forget it, Joey. I told you once before I wasn't that kind of person, and even if I were, you'd be the last person I'd take up with.'

'Yes, I remember, but times and circumstances change, Lexy.'

'No!' She stepped back, but too late. He reached out and drew her to him, forcing her head back, seeking her lips with his. Lexy struggled to evade him, to escape. His arms were like chains binding her to him, his hot breath fanning her face as she arched away from him, kicking him, trying to break free.

'No, Joey. Stop!'

Lexy never quite knew what happened next. One moment she was struggling to escape, the next she was free, staggering to regain her balance at the sudden release. Joey Compton lay on the floor, staring dazedly at the angry visage of the tall man towering above him. Slowly Joey raised himself up on an elbow, his other hand going to his jaw, already swelling.

Lexy wondered wildly if she were dreaming as she watched Dominic flex his right hand, wiggle the fingers; then speak to his cousin.

'If I ever catch you touching her again, I'll beat you bloody. And if I ever hear of you bad-mouthing her in any way, even oblique hints, I'll break you. Is that clear?'

The hard cold voice was one Lexy remembered well, but why was Dominic using it to his cousin? She gazed at him unaware that her heart was in her eyes, her very being.

Joey moved his jaw gingerly, 'Going soft in your old age, Dom?' he asked insolently, eying Lexy.

'Watch what you say, old man, or I'll have you in for defamation of character. That line you've been giving out is all wrong. Sounds like a jealous, spiteful woman, if you ask me,' Dominic bit out.

Lexy was dumbfounded.

'If you can't tell what kind of woman Lexy is, you are dumber than I was.'

Lexy sank in a nearby chair, certain she was dreaming now. Dominic defending her? It was too farfetched; it had to be a dream.

Joey Compton evidently did not agree. He gazed at Dominic for a full minute as realization dawned. He glanced at Lexy, then with an effort he regained his feet prudently putting some distance between him and Dominic.

'Sorry to have misunderstood how things were, Lexy,' he mumbled, 'especially in the circumstances.' He glanced again at his cousin's hard, unyielding face; and, swinging wide to stay out of Dominic's reach, moved to the door. 'See you around, Dom.' He nodded to his cousin and started to leave.

At the door, he paused, turned and looked at Lexy, 'Lexy, I think you would be interested in the dedication page of the book.' Some of his brash cockiness was fast returning. He already was drawing himself up to his full height. Cocking an eyebrow at his cousin, he sketched a salute, 'I do have some family loyalty, Dom.' with that, he left, his feet clattering on the stairs as he descended.

Lexy's head was spinning. Whatever did he mean?

As Dominic crossed to shut the door, she reached out for the book.

She turned the page, and went still. Her breathing stopped; she thought her heart stopped; then it began throbbing. Swallowing hard, she reread the dedication,

For Lexy, with all my love.

For Lexy, with all my love.

Put down in black and white in every copy of his book, for all the world to see. To see and know.

For Lexy, with all my love.

Dear God. Slowly the tears welled up and spilled over, trailing down her cheeks, one to drop on the book, another on the back of her hand. She brushed them away, more came. Dear, darling Dominic. Lexy caught her lip between her teeth, his image blurring as the tears came again. Impatiently she dashed them away, aware through her wavering sight that he was crossing the room, he was coming to her.

She gave a laugh of glee and jumped up to meet him.

'Dominic!'

She flung herself into his arms as he caught her hard against him, sweeping her from the floor, his mouth claiming hers in a long, hard kiss. Lexy reveled in the feel of him, his hair crisp beneath her fingers, the heat and strength of his body passing through her dress, through to her very soul. The tears trickled, she was only aware of Dominic, his mouth, his body, his caressing hands.

Lowering her slowly to the floor, he ended the kiss, moving his mouth across her wet cheeks, to her neck, throat, back to the open softness of her lips. Swinging around a little, he leaned against the wall, drawing her even closer to him, his arms steel bands binding them together.

Reluctantly, slowly, many minutes later, Lexy released his mouth, pulling back just a fraction. 'I'm glad to see you,' she said softly against his lips. 'Would you like to sit down?' Lexy felt if she didn't sit soon, she would melt into a heap at his feet. Her bones felt like water, she was getting light-headed.

Dominic here! Gently, lovingly, kissing her!

Slowly Dominic released her, easing his arms away, his hands trailing from her as if also reluctant to break contact. Standing tall and setting her from him a little, he gave an engaging grin and straightened his tie. Glinting down at her he spoke, 'You got my book.'

For Lexy, with all my love. She smiled mistily, 'Yes!'

She led the way to the sofa, floating on air.

'Sit down,' she said, suddenly shy. 'Can I get you something to drink?'

'Beer, if you have it.' He watched with gentle amusement, knowing she was aware of his barely concealed arousal and flustered by it.

She brought him the beverage and sat near him on the sofa, near but not touching. Dominic cocked a quizzical eyebrow at that.

'I'm so glad you came when you did,' she said breathlessly, 'but how did you know where to find me?' Her eyes were on the foam in his glass.

'I must admit I had a different greeting in mind when I planned to come by. What was Joey doing here?'

'He followed me from work one day and found out where I lived. He was trying his same old routine.' Lexy was anxious to gloss over that part and find out why Dominic was here, how he found her and how, miracle of miracles, he came to believe in her. He had to believe her, or he wouldn't have written that dedication. Wouldn't have showed up out of the blue.

Dominic's expression softened as he gazed at her.

'I don't think we'll be bothered with Joey again.'

She licked her lips. 'You still haven't said how you found me.'

Or why! She thought to herself.

'Private detectives. I was a day late getting to Santa Theresa. Rather than lose you, I called Robin and asked him to engage a detective on my behalf.' He took a long pull on his beer, setting the glass down firmly, and taking her hands in his.

'I was a damned fool. I knew you were telling the truth. I knew long ago that you couldn't have been the kind of girl Joey insinuated. I couldn't help myself, though. I'm most damnably sorry about that scene on the boat, sweetheart. I thought, when you left, maybe you should have some time away from me. So, rather than follow you immediately, like I wanted to do, forcing another confrontation, I waited.' His hands tightened. 'It was so long!'

Lexy was silent, remembering what had almost occurred aboard the Marybeth. She looked up into his face, finding his eyes soft and loving on her. Softly his voice came out, his hands gentle now, caressing.

'How do you think I felt, Lexy? Do you know what I've been through? What hell it was every day thinking of you with all those other men Joey talked about, imagining them touching you, being with you.' He released her hands and drew her closer, fitting her into the crook of his arm, looking deep into her eyes, watching her warily gazing back at him. Slowly his fingers traced from her shoulder down the swell of her breast, his hand cupping her breast, feeling it swell and harden at his touch.

'It just fits,' he whispered, rubbing her slowly, gently with the palm of his hand. Lexy closed her eyes, trembling in love and remembrance. Remembrance of the night on Bob Driscoll's boat when Dominic had said he would make love to her one day.

'What do you think I thought of when Joey was talking on the boat that morning, when he was saying those vile, awful things about you, that he knew and I hadn't even suspected? I wanted to kill him. My own cousin, whom I've known all my life. I wanted to kill him for knowing all those things in your past, for asking you to go off with him. I'm still surprised I didn't beat him to a pulp for telling me.' He shook his head. 'Then today, I just saw red when I came back to see you and found him forcing his attentions on you, trying to kiss –' Dominic trailed off, but Lexy could feel the intense anger still raging in him.

She opened her eyes in surprise; she had never guessed he had felt like that. That he cared so intensely.

'But it wasn't true, at least most of it not true,' she protested, 'and you came in time today. It sounds so corny to say you saved me, but you did.'

She snuggled up to him. He cradled her head, drawing her closer, kissing her soft lips, parting them, probing her mouth with his tongue as his other hand continued its gentle wanderings. Lexy tightened her muscles, moaned a small protest when he moved beneath her bodice to her bare, soft silky skin. Finally he drew back, and took a deep breath.

'I know the things Joey said were lies. I should have known then. But I've been so jealous, my Lexy, so eaten up with it, I thought I should go mad. Imagining you first with Miles Jackson, then his friend Tom, your employer in Santa Inez, the man in England. Even my own cousin.'

She reached her arm up to his shoulder, around his neck bringing her breasts against the hardness of his chest, closing her eyes and offering her mouth in silent, sweet surrender.

'All I could think of,' kissing her eyes, her cheeks, and then he held off for a minute,' was why you didn't wait for me. All my life I've been looking for you, my love, why hadn't you waited for me?'

His hard, exciting kiss woke her from her trance. This was Dominic and he loved her! He had been angry, jealous, but he loved her and wanted her, and she loved him. Forgetting everything but the man in whose arms she lay, Lexy gave herself up to his embrace, reveling in his touch, his kiss, the feel of him against her. His hands were exciting, his mouth giving her such pleasure. Dominic, Dominic, was all Lexy could think of.

When he drew back, breathing hard, to change their position to lie down, Lexy alongside him, she turned her head slightly and kissed his throat. His fingers came beneath her chin, forcing her head up to him. Still feeling shy, she smiled at him. She could feel the warm strong fingers trail down her throat, slip in against her warm skin, caressing her, soothing her. His mouth closed over hers again, his kiss probing, demanding. Lexy was equal to the demand, returning kiss for kiss, until, at last, somewhat assuaged, somewhat less frantic, the kisses became languid and quiet. Lexy moved closer.

'What a waste of time.' Dominic at last pulled back a little. 'I shouldn't have listened to Joey, should have followed my own instincts, still, he made a good case for you as a gold-digger after you fled to the forward cabin. Me a rich, unmarried author, the two of us alone on a deserted island. Sooner or later I'd succumb, then, bang, the big pay-off. Marriage, or maybe just a large settlement to avoid scandal. God forgive me, I believed him. You didn't deny it immediately. I thought you couldn't. Then I enforced that damn rule of not talking about the past. Forgive me, sweetheart, for the lack of trust, for not giving you a chance to explain, to put it all right. I must have hurt you so badly.'

His eyes mirrored some of the pain Lexy had felt during their days together after Joey's malicious revelations. Lexy's heart ached for his own misery, for her remembered hurts and sufferings. She remained silent, what could she say?

She considered the entire situation from Dominic's angle. His cousin was known to him, she had not been, beyond the few days they had traveled together from Santa Inez to Barbados. Yes, he had been cruel and hurtful to her, believing only what Joey had said, denying her a chance to explain, but it had been the wild lashings of a man in pain. It didn't matter now, she realized. It was over, the hurt, the loneliness, the misunderstandings. She loved him and, remarkably so it seemed, he loved her. Her eyes looked up at him in love and forgiveness.

'So my dear, darling Lexy, will you marry me?' he asked whimsically. 'Life will be very much as we've shared on the Marybeth, but with no separate bunks this time. I'll go on locations from time to time to get background material and you can go with me. The rest of the time we'll live on the sloop. Will you take a chance?'

His voice was light, his eyes so serious.

For Lexy, with all my love.

'Yes, please,' she said softly, offering her lips again, happiness and delight flooding through her.

Time drifted by. Lexy had no idea of the hour, but comforted and cherished in their new found love for each other, they talked. She brought him up to date on all the things that had happened to her since that painful scene on the boat; her escape, her coming to Bridgetown, getting her job and running into Joey, leading up to his visit today. Most of it Dominic had already known, from his detective's report.

'I had him keep tabs on you. I would have come in an instant if anything had happened, if you needed help. But I thought, maybe wrongly, we needed some time apart. If only,' he smiled and kissed her nose, 'to appreciate each other more fully when we finally did get together.'

'About Evan,' Dominic began.

'There wasn't anything between us,' Lexy protested quickly.

He sighed. 'I know that. As soon as I realized you had gone, I started thinking. Evan has been talking of coming to the island to dive for years. Always one thing or another kept him from coming. I think the timing was just right for him at that particular juncture, and with the added attraction of a competent and enthusiastic diving partner, he showed up. I was just bringing up everything I could to fight the feeling I had for you. I didn't want to fall in love again.'

'I can understand that. After Harry, I was wary about all men. But you had a happy marriage. Why wouldn't you want another?'

Dominic told her a few things about his life with Marybeth, how he felt that if she'd had to die so young, he was glad it had happened while he still loved her, could remember her with tenderness.

'I was young when we married, young when she died. I wasn't the man then that I am now. Marybeth could never satisfy me now. You and only you, Lexy love, can satisfy me, fill my days with joy and my nights with delight. I'm sorry Marybeth died, but I don't think our marriage would have lasted, were she alive today.' Lexy gave a brief passing regret for the unfortunate Marybeth. She would never come between Lexy and Dominic. Lexy was sorry she had died so young, but so glad Dominic was free now and wanted her!

He told her how he had persuaded his publisher to rush over the first book off the press, so that he could give it to her, to show her he loved her, to make the way for him to hope against hope she felt the same.

They were still exchanging confidences when darkness fell. Lexy suggested a light supper and went to start it while Dominic called Robin to tell him he was eating at Lexy's; and to pass on the news Robin and Sarah had been anticipating.

He joined her in the small kitchen.

'I asked Robin to call Aunt Patience for me,' he said, coming over and kissing her neck as she prepared their omelets.

'What?'

'To tell her that I am marrying you first chance I get.'

She beamed up at him, happiness and love shining from her eyes. 'And when will that be?'

'Not before morning, anyway. We'll see about the marriage license then.'

'And in the mean time?' she asked casually, her eyes on the pan.

'In the mean time Robin has a nice bed that I hope I have to sleep on only once more.' He encircled her waist, drawing her back against his chest, breathing in her perfume, kissing her gently on the cheek.

'I love you, Lexy.'

'Oh, Dominic, I love you so much! It was a beautiful thing you wrote in your book. I'll always treasure it.'

They were married two days later, in Bridgetown; Robin and Sarah standing witness. They welcomed Lexy gladly to the family. After a short wedding breakfast all together, Dominic and Lexy had returned to the privacy of her flat for a few days of solitude.

Loving and laughing, talking and planning, happy and content, they began their married days together. The shadow laid by Joey Compton so long ago banished forever. Lexy bloomed in her new found happiness, love shining from her, happiness welling up and spilling over. Her life was almost too good to be true.

Two mornings later, at breakfast, Dominic dropped two sheets of paper at Lexy's place as he bent to kiss her again. They had been up for quite a while, but were only just now starting breakfast. She looked up rosy-cheeked and happy, a slight question in her eyes? 'What's this?'

'Read them,' he invited.

One was a filled-out form for sending cables, the other a reply cablegram.

'Alexander Kentfield, Larchmont Tower, Brayford, Dorset, England. Have married your granddaughter Stop Passing through England soon Stop Shall we call Stop Reply, Dominic Frazer, 7 Grenache Street, Bridgetown Barbados, W.I.'

Lexy's eyes were swimming in tears as she read the reply.

'Dominic Frazer, 7 Grenache Street, Bridgetown, Barbados, W.I. Have searched for years Stop All forgiven this end Stop Can Lexy forgive her end Stop Warm welcome in England. Stop Please come. Alexander Kentfield.'

Dominic raised his wife's face, searching her tear-filled eyes. 'Shall we honeymoon in England?' he asked her softly.

She nodded, love swelling her heart almost to bursting. 'Thank you, my love.'

The long dark years were over. Lexy had come into the sun.

If you liked **Come Into The Sun**,
you'll love book 3 in the Tropical Escape series,
Island Paradise.

You can find all Barbara McMahon's books
on her website at barbaramcmahon.com.

www.ingramcontent.com/pod-product-compliance
Lightning Source LLC
Chambersburg PA
CBHW060936180626
46817CB00004B/1578